Hitler's Will

Greg Causey

Copyright © 2009 Romance Divine LLC
ISBN 978-1-934446-67-6
Cover Design by Grigori

Published by
Romance Divine
www.romancedivine.com

For
Our Fathers

WWII Veterans

Dale K Causey,
U.S. Army Air Corps

&

Robert E. Rolls,
U.S. Army

Hitler's Will

Greg Causey

You only know those
who cause you suffering.
Johann Wolfgang Von Goethe
Maxim 845

One

Berlin, The *Führerbunker*
28 April 1945

They were reducing his beloved Berlin to rubble. *SS* Major Jürgen Strasser huddled beneath the arches of the *Brandenburger Tor*, the incessant Russian artillery fire pounding the city, shaking the very earth. He glanced up the street to see the once-elegant *Unter den Linden* filled with wreckage, cars, parts of buildings, smoldering heaps of death and destruction. Here and there a lone figure darted among the ruins seeking shelter from the onslaught.

Madness, it's over, we've lost! And I've been sent on a fool's errand. He was *SS*, a veteran of six years of brutal fighting, storming through France with Guderian's Panzers and narrowly slipping through the noose that ensnared *von Paulus's* 6th Army at Stalingrad, surviving while those around him died. His latest assignment was cryptic: "Proceed immediately to Berlin. You will be met at the Chancellery and taken to the *Führerbunker*." These simple, direct, and terse orders had been signed by none other than Otto Skorzney, and Strasser's duty as a soldier was to follow orders.

He huddled against the stone edifice as a barrage of Russian *Katyusha* rockets shrieked overhead, lacking in accuracy but fearsome and deadly, wreaking havoc as they landed in the *Tiergarten*. Their banshee screams sent the Berliners running for cover just as the wail of the *Stukas* did the Poles in 1939. *Stalin's Organs, retribution for our sins of war*. He ran the last hundred meters to the Chancellery. He didn't know who he was supposed to meet, when, or where; he simply had his orders.

Near the corner of the Chancellery he came upon a Hitler Youth detachment manning a small machine gun position. *Cannon fodder, they don't stand a chance against the Russian tanks that will soon be here.*

The Sergeant in command of the position checked his papers and led him into the bombed-out Chancellery. The building mimicked the world around him. Once a seat of power to intimidate foreign officials it was now empty, windows broken, papers strewn about, the former exquisite crystal chandeliers now reduced to twinkling shards of glass to be trod upon by both victor and vanquished.

Inside the building Strasser was taken to a staircase. Following the stairs down to the Butler's Pantry, he was greeted by two *SS* guards who opened a steel door and ushered him in. Down another flight of stairs and through the corridors he found himself in the bowels of the bunker, under the Chancellery garden. Again, his papers were checked and he was told to wait in one of the many small cubicles that made up the underground labyrinth.

A middle-aged woman stopped and offered ersatz coffee, short of any real taste or flavor, but warm and drinkable. Her face was gaunt, her eyes hollow, darkened circles of fear and despair. She nervously looked around to see if they were alone. In hushed, low tones she asked, "*Herr* Major, General Wenck and the XII Army, they are coming to relieve us?"

Wearily Major Strasser shook his head. "I know of no relief, *Gnadige Frau*."

For the briefest moment her eyes twinkled, a faint smile turned up the corners of her lips, she couldn't remember when someone last called her 'Gracious Lady'. Then the hopelessness set in; her shoulders fell, and she sighed. Without meeting his eyes again she turned and left.

After an hour he was met by Martin Bormann, who perfunctorily checked his papers and told him to wait yet longer.

The time passed slowly, and the rumbling impacts of the Russian bombardment could be felt, even in the relative safety of the bunker three meters below ground. Bits of dust and cement fell from the ceiling lending a hazy, ethereal pall to the starkness of the underground refuge. He waited as people passed by, working, talking in low, hushed tones. He saw famed test pilot Hanna Reitsch with a *Luftwaffe* General he didn't recognize. Reitsch, fearless as a test pilot, was visibly distraught, clutching a bundle of letters tightly in her hand.

He waited. The relentless droning of the ventilation system had an almost hypnotic effect. He badly wanted a cigarette, but smoking wasn't permitted; the *Führer* didn't approve of the habit. Someone brought him a sandwich, it was good to have food, but otherwise he was ignored. He closed his eyes and pondered the last six years. He'd joined the *SS* shortly after the German-Polish incident in 1939 that plunged the world into war. For six years he'd fought hard, led his men and watched most die. Had he been more of a politician, and less of a warrior, he may have advanced further than Major. God knows he'd seen lesser men, not leaders or warriors like himself, progress past him up the ranks. He was a fighter, not a talker or schemer, which meant that this current assignment needed someone who got results, someone who did the dirty work.

Stalingrad had been the worst, the vaunted 6th Army encircled by the Soviet forces. He remembered the cold day in January 1943, in the ruins of a Russian department store, the last headquarters of General Friedrich *von* Paulus. The General turned to him, holding a message. "Strasser, the *Führer* has promoted me to Field Marshal."

"Congratulations *Mein* General, it is long overdue."

"Ha! He intends me to fight to the death; no German Field Marshal has ever surrendered. Strasser, the situation here is hopeless, but the Fatherland still needs men like you. Take what men you can, those who can still move and fight, and break out, tonight. It must be tonight, tomorrow will be too late."

That night Strasser and a handful of men made their way through the Russian lines and the next day General *von* Paulus surrendered the 6th Army. The next two years found Strasser leading his men in a continuing series of hopeless holding actions and retreats.

I've spent three days again crossing Russian lines, risking my life to come to Berlin and what—wait? Watch?

His thoughts were broken by the adjutant standing before him. "The *Führer* will see you now."

Strasser stood, ran his hands through his hair and tugged at the wrinkled battle tunic he wore. There was no way he could make himself look presentable.

The adjutant led Major Strasser out of the cubicle and down the corridor. The artillery rumbled overhead, the ventilation system droned, and he was going to meet the *Führer*.

For what? What? This is madness, sheer madness.

Twenty minutes later Strasser followed Bormann to the bunker's emergency exit. Strasser's hand patted the pocket of his battle tunic, ensuring the safety of the precious package from the *Führer*.

Bormann turned to give Strasser his last instructions. "Your best chance through the Russian lines is west through the *Tiergarten*. You can cross the *Havel* River on the *Charlottenbrücken*." He handed Strasser a set of orders. "This allows you to commandeer whatever transport and supplies you may need; when you complete your mission form up with General Tolsdorff. He is organizing *Wehrmacht*, *Luftwaffe* and *SS* units in the Berchtesgaden and *Obersalzberg* areas. *Heil Hitler und Viel Gluck.*"

Strasser emerged to a landscape of destruction. Outside, explosions echoed throughout the city; tracer rounds and flames piercing the night sky. Against the flames, billowing ashen clouds dissolved into the blackness above, funeral pyres consuming a culture. Strasser immediately turned and headed west. *It's a living hell, Götterdämmerung. They haven't killed me in six years and not today, maybe tomorrow.*

Two

The *Obersalzberg*
Present Day

The dampness was palpable. Otto Schleiman felt it on his skin, smelled the dank, moldy scent of it, tasted it in his mouth as the sweat dripped down his face. He trudged through the dimly lit corridor, his tall frame stooping in deference to the stalactites descending from the tunnel ceiling. His steps echoed before and behind him, his feet splashing in the small pools of water that collected on the coarse and uneven concrete floor. It was nearly fifty meters before he stopped in the passage and turned to his left to face the large orange rectangle on the wall. In the stillness of the underground labyrinth the lacquer smell still hung in the air, although Schleiman had painted it there yesterday. These conditions didn't concern him. Scientists, explorers and archaeologists had to endure such things in their quest for the great discoveries. Schleiman felt he was all of those, on the verge of a great discovery.

He placed the canvas bag and the electric lantern on the floor. To be certain, he pulled his cell phone out of his pocket and checked. Just as he thought; there was no signal, not inside the mountain, inside the bunker, not inside the last redoubt. He remembered his last conversation with his colleague, Karl Kessler…

"Karl! I've found it, the location, I've got it!" exclaimed Schleiman over the cell phone outside the small *Gästehaus* in Berchtesgaden. "I'm sure of it. I marked it. It's there, I know it."

"We must be certain. I'll be there tomorrow, the day after at the latest."

"Time is critical, there may be others, we need to be the first."

"Otto, please, let me do this, you're a scientist. I'm the engineer. The tunnels are old and dangerous."

"Hurry, get here and you'll see. I'll show it to you. It must be done, quickly."

Schleiman brought his thoughts back to the matters at hand. He went to work with the hammer and chisel, cutting along the orange lines, as if he were carving out a door in the stone. *I am*, he mused, *a portal to fame, academic and scholarly acclaim. The name Otto Schleiman will be ranked alongside that of Heinrich Schleiman, the discoverer of the lost city of Troy*. Otto, however, was after a different treasure, not as ancient, but just as astounding to the world.

The tunnel slowly filled with dust and debris from his stone cutting and stuck to his sweaty skin. Still, he continued, fueled by the desire to get to the treasure he was certain lay on the other side. He thought for a moment and laughed at the televised debacle of that pompous American newsman who opened up 'Al Capone's Secret Vaults' on live American TV. Unfortunately Schleiman's discovery would be made in secret before it could be revealed publicly. He choked on more of the dust and washed it down with a lukewarm bottle of *Gerolsteiner* water.

He'd thought the sound would be hollow; instead it sounded as if he hammered on solid rock and concrete. He'd checked and rechecked the distances, the coordinates, even using one of the new GPS units to accurately fix and verify the locations above ground. The passage was there, he was sure of it. *This has to be it.*

Satisfied with his mini excavation on the wall he pushed the plastic explosive, using all the dangerous material he had, into the cracks around the door, his portal to fame. He inserted the detonator and began uncoiling the wire, backing away the length of the tunnel.

Patience is a critical trait, important to scientist and archaeologist alike and, in his past, Otto Schleiman had been a good and patient scientist. Today however, he was flushed with the adrenalin of discovery. *Will another fifty or one hundred meters really make that much difference?*

Schleiman stopped, stripped back the wires and fixed them to the control unit. He turned his back to the direction from where he'd come and hunched over. *Tomorrow,* he thought, *tomorrow another Schleiman, another discoverer of antiquities will be famous. Soon they will read about me in the newspapers.* He smiled and turned the handle. The roar was deafening, the tunnel shook. He saw…blackness.

Three

Patrick Deveraux took another drink of his *Weizen* Beer and set the glass down. He gazed at the small story buried in the back of the *Frankfurt Allegmagne*:

Univeristät Archeologist Killed
in Tunnel Collapse
70 year-old, retired university professor Otto Schleiman found buried in the debris of a tunnel collapse while doing research work on the *Obersalzberg*.

The story didn't give any details of why Schleiman had been poking around the old tunnels of the *Obersalzberg* or what he was researching. *Probably another Nazi treasure hunter looking for loot or some angle to promote a book deal.*

Patrick sat back and brought the beer to his lips. It was a beautiful spring day in *München* and the *Marienplatz* was the perfect place to enjoy it. The sun had moved, and the umbrella at his table no longer provided him shade, but he didn't mind the sun and sat back to enjoy its warmth. Two women strolled arm-in-arm along the street. They were stylishly dressed, one wearing an expensive reptile print leather vest. It made him think of his beloved Heike. Four years ago he would have spent this day with her. They would have enjoyed a light lunch and beers. She would have slipped her feet out of her high-heeled sandals to playfully…

"*Herr* Deveraux?"

The stranger standing in front of Patrick interrupted his melancholic reverie. He'd noticed him earlier, across the *Marienplatz*, seemingly there, waiting, not exactly out of place, but still, somehow, out of context. *Old habits die hard, and I'm getting sloppy sitting here daydreaming and being surprised like this.*

Patrick slowly placed his glass on the coaster and benignly nodded at the visitor. He sensed that the interloper spoke English and replied, "Yes, I'm Patrick Deveraux." Even while he nonchalantly made his salutation his eyes scanned the crowd. *Is he alone? Did he come with friends, followers, handlers?* None to his surprise the visitor replied in perfect English.

"*Herr* Deveraux, if I may sit and have a word with you?"

Patrick silently nodded to an empty chair. The stranger was dressed in a well-cut, dark European suit with high lapels. With his medium height and build, receding hairline, and round wire-framed glasses he appeared almost professorial, or perhaps a chartered accountant. He may have looked rather unassuming, but Patrick noted a studied economy in his motions, his posture, the way he handled himself. This was someone to be wary of, not to be taken lightly. *What's going on? It's a nice day in Munich and I'm enjoying a beer. Why are these old habits kicking in? That's not who I am—now.*

"…..on a day like today, isn't it?"

The stranger's voice brought Patrick back to his senses. "Excuse me?"

His visitor smiled a business-like 'let me show you our new product' kind of smile. "I said that it's a beautiful day to relax on the *Marienplatz,* is it not?"

Patrick smiled in return, a better smile, one that reflected something of his father's roguish Irish charm. Patrick raised his glass, "Yes, a sunny day, a good beer, a street full of beautiful women and happy children."

The visitor nodded, "Yes, of course. *Herr* Deveraux, if I may please have a moment to discuss something of a business nature, a proposition of temporary employment perhaps?"

It was best now to listen and observe, to scan the environment and stop the daydreaming. Patrick realized this person didn't simply stumble onto him. He, or they, had either been looking for him, or planned to find him here. The *Marienplatz* was a good place to be, and he was often found here by friends.

The visitor continued. "My name is Walter King. I represent a consortium who would like you to procure something for us. You are, I understand, a person who has the experience and facility to do such things, or this is what we have been led to believe." King studied the man seated across from him. This Patrick Deveraux was older than the one in the photograph given to King. Deveraux's brown hair was graying at the edges now, there were more lines around his eyes. Yet the eyes were the same, dark and flat, seeing everything and revealing nothing, certainly not laughing Irish eyes. He was taller than King, and seemed fit, though certainly not possessing an action-hero's muscular body. To King he looked much like any man one might pass on the street, dressed conservatively in slacks, polo shirt and sport coat.

Patrick tried to place the accent, mid-Atlantic? The diction was very precise. He smiled warmly and took another sip of his beer. It was nearly empty and he planned to enjoy yet another before the day was through. He caught the waiter's eye, *"Bitte, Herr Oberst, ein mal bitte,"* he held up the nearly empty glass. The waiter nodded and Patrick returned the glass to the coaster. He looked at his guest, "I'm an antiques dealer, if that's what you mean."

King smiled back and opened a small leather notebook. "More of a second-hand furniture operation although, yes, you do sell the occasional antique. I believe that in the past you have enjoyed, shall we say, *other* means of support."

"The operation, as you call it, was something owned by my wife and I. I've continued to run it after her death."

"Yes, the *Autobahn* accident four years ago was untimely and lamentable. It is hard to lose a loved one, is it not?"

OK, he knows too much for this to simply be a casual business deal. Patrick's searching eyes finally found the thing that was out of place. The same Audi sedan had circled the block three times, finally parking across the street with a view of the two of them. The second beer came and Patrick nodded his thanks.

"Mr. King, I'm really not looking to expand, or for anything else. I buy and sell a few things; it gives me time to sit here in the afternoons and drink my beer, read my paper, and watch the people."

"Of course *Herr* Deveraux, but you've not yet heard my offer."

Patrick tipped his glass in King's direction, "Go ahead, I'm listening."

King cast a glance at the newspaper on the table. "The tragic incident on the *Obersalzberg*, we would like you to look into that."

Patrick set down his glass and picked up the newspaper. "A dead archeologist? I'm not a reporter, detective or an investigator. I run a second hand furniture store. Remember?"

"*Herr* Schleiman was looking for something. He may have found it, or knew where it was. We would like *you* to obtain it for us."

Both men were silent for a moment, the polite niceties now concluded.

Deliberately, and never taking his eyes from Walter King, Patrick placed the newspaper on the table and leaned forward. "I'm not a treasure hunter, or messenger service."

King held up a hand, palm facing Patrick in a conciliatory gesture. "Of course, my apologies, I've been vague and evasive. What I tell you now is, of course, highly confidential and should you decline our offer—"

"Mr. King, if I hear your proposal and don't accept your offer, then you and your concerns were just a passing moment in my day, soon to be forgotten."

King's lips curled into a feral smile. "What they say about you, your reputation, is as we would have expected."

Casting furtive glances around the table, King leaned in and whispered, "Schleiman was searching for Hitler's Last Will and Testament." He sat back in his chair and looked around, fearful that someone may have heard.

He made no response, but Patrick's body shook as he attempted to stifle a chuckle. *Another treasure hunter on a fool's errand.*

King was not amused; he leaned in again, his voice more hushed than before. "You think perhaps we are *Odessa*, or *Skorzeny's* Werewolves? We are not! But our clients have their own reasons for wanting the true document."

Patrick took another drink of his beer. It was good beer; even a bad conversation couldn't spoil a good beer. His finger wiped away the drops of condensation on the glass and watched as the Friar holding the beer tankard came into view. He leaned back, a pensive look on his face as he tried to recall the details. "The exact specifics elude me, but it's my recollection that Hitler dictated his Last Will and Testament to his secretary on, what was it, 28 April?"

"29 April," Walter King replied dryly.

With a 'so what' shrug Patrick continued. "And it was witnessed by Goebbels, Bormann and some others I can't remember."

King nodded his agreement.

"And... Hitler threw Göring and Himmler out of the Nazi party, picked Dönitz and Goebbels to run things, left some art to his hometown of Linz." Patrick fixed King with a steely glare. "So what? It's old history."

"Old history and wrong history, *Herr* Deveraux; there was a second Will and Testament, the *real one*."

Patrick expelled a breath of air as if he were weary from the conversation. "Look, I'm not an expert, but I know a bit about history; it helps when you deal in antiques. I've never read anywhere, not in Toland, not in Roper, Shirer, or any of the writers about a second, *true* Will."

"Have you ever heard of Major Jürgen Strasser?"

Patrick shook his head 'no' and reached for the beer. This one was almost gone. If this conversation didn't wrap up soon he was going to need another.

"Strasser was *SS*, tough and loyal, personally picked by Otto Skorzeny for one last mission at the end of the war. He was seen at the *Führerbunker* on the 28th and 29th of April 1945, took a personal meeting with Hitler, after which he vanished. We have reason to believe that he was given the genuine Last Will and Testament."

Quiet now, Patrick listened. Often it was better to let the other person talk; silence usually prompted someone to speak.

King continued. "We are offering you 250,000 Euros for the recovery of this document." He withdrew an envelope from his jacket and placed it on the table. "This contains 50,000 Euros for, shall we say, a retainer and expenses."

"And your clients? They are…"

"None of your business *Herr* Deveraux. The money buys your services, the delivery of the merchandise-and their anonymity."

Patrick drained his beer and set the empty glass on the table. "You realize there is little chance that such a document exists. I think you're wasting my time, and your money. You remember the fiasco with the Hitler diaries and *Stern* magazine in the eighties?"

King smiled thinly, reassured that every man has a price. He dropped his business card on top of the envelope.

"When you have the document you can contact me and I will tell you where to deliver it." He stood to leave.

Patrick slipped the envelope in his pocket. "For the record, I don't believe there's another Will. I don't think I'll find anything."

Walter King buttoned his jacket. "Background information and contacts are in the envelope. When you have delivered the document we will transfer the remaining money into a numbered Swiss Account of your choosing." With a curt bow and an "*Auf Weidersehen*," King turned and walked across the *Marienplatz* to the waiting Audi. A second man held the rear door open as King slid in. As the car left the square King watched Patrick Deveraux slowly fade into the distance.

*****

"What now?" Kurt asked from the front of the car.

King looked out the window. "We find the document."

"But that's what you hired Deveraux to do."

"That's who the client wants. Our Arab friend wants both the document and to settle an old score with Deveraux. To the client we're middle-men, faceless cut-outs, fucking intermediaries." King spat out the last words derisively.

The others were silent. King was the leader; they simply followed orders and got paid.

King continued, "Regardless of who the client wants, all he's really interested in is the Will and Deveraux's death. We get the package and we make our own deal—for a lot more than we're being paid."

The man beside King spoke up, "What if Deveraux gets the package? Do we arrange the meeting between him and the client as planned?"

King sighed in frustration; the delineation between brains and muscle in his group was painfully obvious. "If Deveraux gets the package we take it from him and make our own deal with the client. Deveraux goes back to his little second-hand shop—or ends up dead."

From the front of the car, Horst spoke up. "Maybe, I don't know, it might not be that easy. Deveraux, some say he was an IRA assassin."

That's why I do the planning and thinking. "I'm taking some insurance to keep *Herr* Deveraux in line," King said. "I'm sending Kurt to Hamburg. He'll make sure our interests are served and keep Deveraux in check. And if we need more help there are always the Stuber brothers."

There was a general mumbling of agreement to the plan. "So what now?" Kurt asked.

"We question the engineer, *Herr* Kessler, in Berlin."

*****

Patrick watched the Audi drive away. King's story was dubious at best; he didn't believe half of it, nor did he trust King. There was, however, no doubting the 50,000 Euros; he patted the envelope in his pocket and signaled the waiter for another beer. While waiting, he picked up his cell phone to call Hannelore.

ﬀour

A pool of sweat and tears gathered under the leather blindfold making Andreas's eyes burn. His right hamstring cramped, but securely fastened across the leather spanking horse there was no hope of relief.

Leather cuffs on each wrist and ankle kept him tightly tethered and spread. A leather collar and chain connected to the floor prevented him from raising his head. The chains across his back, further binding and restricting him, had lost their frightening chill from their first application, directly from Mistress Hannelore's freezer. "*Es ist Kalt?*" she had mocked.

Yes, Andreas thought, *it IS fucking cold!* Now he was alone in the dark, quiet room with his reddened eyes, cramping muscles and the gruesome welts on his ass.

Mistress Hannelore was an artist, able to paint a collage of welts, bruises and red splotches that would find a home in any collection of avant-garde art. Her client had no idea what time it was. She not only toyed with his body, she manipulated his mind, altering his very concepts of time and space. That's why she cost 500 Euros an hour and was very selective about her clients.

Andreas tried to relax, to find his place, his center, let the energy flow out of him and dissipate. *Where is she? What's coming next? Breathe and feel each breath, let the pain become color and heat, let it out.* Footsteps, the precise clicks of her stiletto-heeled boots on the cold, hard floor echoed in her dungeon. He heard her; felt her presence as she circled him, and caught the scent of her as she passed.

CRACK! The leather riding crop exploded against his exposed backside. Just as suddenly she used it to trace a loving line down his spine, and his body folded softly into the sensation. She tormented him with this inanimate leather extension of her being, using the crop to coax any number of responses from him.

CRACK! She struck that tender spot between the upper thighs and buttocks. The pain seared through him. He cringed and tried to relax. Again, it came, the soft caress of the leather.

"Did you miss me, *Liebchen*? I was here, watching you, enjoying your suffering and confusion. It feels wonderful does it not, to give up all, to yield, to submit?"

She grabbed his hair, running her talon-like nails through it, grazing his scalp. Her lips broke into a soft smile as she attacked the delicate and sensitive skin. In a distant room her phone softly rang, her personal line; the answering machine picked up and recorded the message.

She released his head, perhaps a bit too violently. That's what Andreas wanted, what they all wanted, why they paid the 500 Euros; and she always gave them their money's worth, always.

She walked to the wall and hung the exquisite leather crop on a hook. Eyeing the array of instruments, she selected a wicked leather whip, a cat-of-nine-tails. She hefted it in her hand, changing the position and grip until she found that sweet spot, a balance she could appreciate.

The leather tails of the cat unwound with a sound that thrilled her—and brought panic to her clients. She saw Andreas wince, knowing he was aware of what was to come, that he hated it, yet he desired it desperately, a desire that had become a need. *A paradox,* she thought, *that must drive them insane.*

She let the cat dangle and moved her wrist just enough so he heard the rippling of the leather tails as she approached him. Her nails ran across his back, a tender prelude to the final crescendo of pain she was about to unleash. "Almost done," she cooed. "You've done well. I wouldn't waste my time with someone not worth it."

She attacked him with the cat. From his calves to his upper back she was relentless and creative. She struck three quick blows to the same place, multiplying the sensation. As his battered body registered the pain from the first stroke the second landed. The onslaught was overwhelming for Andreas. He struggled to focus, to maintain, but her skills were too much for him. She read his body language, his breathing, his guttural responses and moans. Before he could get control she would wrest it from him with a vicious attack that confused him. When it was over both were bathed in sweat. Hannelore walked to the wall and hung up the cat.

Hannelore waited, giving them each a moment to regroup before she went to him and removed the blindfold. She stroked his cheeks and bent down, planting a small kiss on each tear-stained eyelid, her Chanel lipstick leaving its trademark imprint. Her clients carried this away as a badge of honor.

"You did well, Mistress is pleased. I enjoyed our time, *Liebchen*. Katja will see to your needs. *Bis Später*."

Hannelore turned on her heels and left the dungeon, beckoning her submissive, Katja, to see to the client's after-care needs. When she reached her bedroom she disrobed, catching her reflection in the mirror, pleased with what she saw. Hannelore possessed a natural, Teutonic beauty, not sweet California girly, but a real Norse woman's face and figure. Free of her stiletto boots she still stood an imposing five feet ten. She loosened her hair from its austere Domina bun and let it fall, a dark brunette mane that flowed to her shoulders, framing a face whose main attraction were haunting brown eyes. Even in her mid-40s she was a formidable woman, attractive, with an authoritative confidence that captivated both men and women alike. After washing her face, she settled into the corner chair with her feet on the ottoman and reached for the telephone remote to play back her messages.

"Hannelore, it's Patrick. I'm coming up to Hamburg on the train. I've taken a contract for some work in Berlin and here in Bavaria. I'll stop in and see you on my way to Berlin. I'll call you tonight with the details. We can do dinner at the *Ratsweinkeller*."

She leaned back in the chair and smiled. Patrick was coming, how wonderful! It was always good to see him, to see family.

Katja quietly entered the room and knelt before Mistress Hannelore, who reclined in graceful repose. It was now time for Hannelore's after-care. Katja positioned her lithe body between Mistress's thighs and planted loving kisses on her fragrant sex. Yes, sometimes the sessions did excite Hannelore, but sex with a client? Never! Strictly *Verbotten*! Yet she always got hers, and now she softly moaned as Katja's mouth languidly lapped at her sex.

Hannelore reached down, grabbing the girl's head, pulling her closer, smearing the juices from her fiery slit over Katja's soft face.

Katja pressed against Mistress's sex and fed ravenously. Her nimble fingers gently pulled away Hannelore's nether lips, her tongue plowing deep into the moist cavern. That cat-like tongue found Hannelore's clit and Katja sucked it between her lips, gently pulling and kneading the throbbing nub.

Mistress Hannelore arched her back, grabbing Katja by the hair as she held the head tightly between her legs. *Katja, my sweet little Katja.* Hannelore pulled harder, crushing Katja's face into her sex. As she came, she shuddered and pushed Katja away. When Hannelore relaxed, Katja crawled forward again to lick her Mistress clean, softly, gently, like a kitten lapping up milk.

The sated Dominatrix relaxed and sighed. Life was good. And Patrick was coming, how wonderful! *Patrick kommen. Wunderbar!*

*****

Hannelore stirred under the warmth of the heavy comforter. Katja nestled closer, her small, but firm breasts pressed against Hannelore's back. She felt Katja's lips plant a tender kiss on her neck as they snuggled in the bed. Outside the apartment Hamburg was coming to life, although in her up-scale *Blankenese* neighborhood the noise was less. Hannelore glanced at the clock. She had no clients this morning and Patrick was not arriving until the evening; she would sleep a bit longer.

Half an hour later she felt Katja gently slide from the bed, on her way to the kitchen to make coffee. Hannelore rose and slipped on a red, silk robe. Lighting her first cigarette of the day, she entered her office and made a quick check of the Bremen, Hamburg and Frankfurt stock exchanges. Hannelore didn't intend to Dom professionally forever, nor did she intend to retire in poverty. Among her clientele were businessmen, lawyers and investors who paid her well, and counseled her well. Katja returned with the coffee and knelt on the floor while Hannelore affectionately stroked the young girl's hair.

Hannelore tried to concentrate on her financials but couldn't focus on the numbers on the screen. She was thinking of last night's conversation with Patrick: thousands of Euros, lost Nazi documents, 60-year old secrets; it was a bad business, dangerous. She pushed Katja gently away, stood and began to pace the room.

She knew Patrick was competent, even dangerous, but she worried. When he and Heike made their new lives he'd left his mercenary ways behind, or so she'd thought. With Heike gone Hannelore didn't intend to lose another loved one. She lit another cigarette. Now Patrick was back in the game, embarking on another dangerous adventure, the kind of business that required equally hard and dangerous men. She gently tugged on Katja's hair, "Get Dieter on the phone."

*****

The water was moderately choppy and the fog light as Dieter Falke brought his fishing boat, *Der Norde Stern*, up the River Elbe into Hamburg. The North Star was a small fishing boat, but Dieter didn't rely on fishing as a living. He enjoyed the freedom of the sea and the challenge of the elements; Dieter was a born skipper, the one in command. Yet he'd cut this trip short because Hannelore called and asked for his help; and who could refuse Hannelore anything? As he passed the *Blankenese* district he glanced to port. *Is Hannelore awake? And Katja?*

He pulled off his fisherman's cap, pushed his blond hair out of the way and put the cap back on. Dieter shifted his weight, flexed his knees and stretched to his full six foot five height; the damp sea air wasn't good for his knee. The doctor had reconstructed the knee and recommended during rehabilitation that Dieter move inland, away from the cold and damp. But fishing was Dieter's second occupation of choice.

He glanced down in the cabin to see Mathias asleep, the sheet half covering his naked body. "Mathias! We tie up soon."

The naked form stirred, Mathias raising his head. Even with a bad case of bed hair, his curly black hair and deep black eyes looked like something cherubic from a Renaissance painting.

As Mathias dressed, Dieter guided the boat up river, noting the channel buoys and oncoming freighter traffic. They'd tie up at the wharf, get some rest and then see Hannelore.

Scanning the river ahead his eyes stopped for a moment on the tattered and weather-beaten photograph tacked above the ship's wheel. The photograph showed five men posing before a burned-out Mercedes sedan. All of the men were dressed in black and held MP5 SD3s, the silenced versions. Their torsos were clad in body armor and tactical vests adorned with the accoutrements of counterinsurgency warfare. Dark camouflage obscured their faces and black stocking caps covered their heads. They were serious looking men, dealers of death. Anyone looking at the picture was immediately drawn to the tall one in the center, who rose above the others, the one with the cold gray eyes and the shock of blond hair falling from the stocking cap.

He thought about the phone call with Hannelore, her request to help a friend, family, watch his back. Dieter reached into a drawer, removed a canvas package and dumped the edged weapons on a nearby chart table. He dropped the KM2000 German combat knife in the pocket of his coat.

He grabbed the Sykes-Fairbairn commando knife, held it in his hand, reacquainting himself with the feel, the balance. Suddenly he turned, the knife flying from his hand towards the stern of the boat. Just as suddenly, without seeing where the knife struck, Dieter returned his attention to guiding the boat up-river.

Mathias emerged from the cabin and made his way to the stern. His eyes saw the knife buried deep into the fist-sized, red-painted heart on the gunwale.

Five

Patrick took the Euros from the girl in the kiosk and shoved them in his pocket. He quickly scanned the headline of the *Bild* newspaper and the bare-chested, buxom blonde on the front before folding it under his arm. *You'd never see that in the States.*

He grabbed his bag and walked into the sprawling *München Bahnhof*. The train ride from *München* to Hamburg would take several hours, but he didn't mind, he'd read his paper; have some lunch and a few drinks; he liked traveling by train.

The sleek train lay on the silver tracks, a giant armored snake, fast and lethal. He quickly found his seat and settled in. Gazing out the window, he watched the activity, people arriving and leaving on the other trains.

His mind drifted back to yesterday's conversation at the *Marienplatz* and the subsequent events…

Patrick hadn't lived so long by being careless. After his

meeting with Walter King he changed the passwords on the security systems and computers at both his apartment and his antiques shop and ran virus scans on both. A quick check of his recent bank transactions revealed nothing suspicious. Nothing seemed amiss; all was in order. Still, Walter King had good information about him. Patrick would err on the side of caution; it's what had kept him alive while others around him died.

He poured himself two shots of Jameson's and reflected on his current situation. The last four years, since Heike's death, he'd simply gone through the motions: denial, grief, running the shop, drinking at the *Marienplatz*. Before that he'd been a mercenary of sorts, a part-time IRA assassin. He'd left his past behind and Heike had filled the void, she'd been his life, and with her gone? He shook off the gloomy thoughts. Now he had a job, such as it was.

What was his job? Find a 60-year old document that no one knew existed? He didn't believe in the job—or in his employer, Mr. Walter King. He did believe in the fifty thousand Euros in the envelope.

Tomorrow he'd take the train to Hamburg to see Hannelore, but first he'd do a little research. After a quick bratwurst and a beer at a neighborhood *Imbiss* he walked to the underground station; it was only a short *U-Bahn* ride to visit an old friend.

Bruno Wenz was a WWII *Luftwaffe* pilot, an ace with fifty-six kills and later a Colonel in the post-war German Air Force. He'd earned most of his kills in *Messerschmitt 109's*, but preferred the radial-engined *Focke Wulf 190's* he flew in the waning days of the war. As Heike's uncle he'd formed a close relationship with Patrick. They saw in each other the noble warrior, the soldier, albeit in different times and roles. While Heike never saw it, both he and Bruno saw the killer in each other.

Now in his eighties Bruno's mind was still sharp; he was on his computer everyday e-mailing people, researching and writing. He was an amateur historian, and the most immediate and best resource available to Patrick.

Bruno greeted Patrick warmly, graciously accepting the bottle of brandy brandished by his guest. He ushered Patrick into a house that was neat and organized with Teutonic efficiency. Bruno set the bottle on a table crafted from the horizontal stabilizer of a P-51 Mustang and pulled two crystal glasses from a cabinet.

While Bruno poured the drinks, Patrick's practiced eye took in the shelves of books, boxes of photos and mementos.

Taking a chair opposite Patrick, Bruno handed him a glass. They took a moment to study the amber-colored liquid before clicking glasses.

"May we attend our enemy's funerals," Patrick proffered.

A laughing Bruno replied, "*Prost!*"

They drank in silence.

Bruno was the first to speak. "It's good to see you, Patrick. What brings you here, although you are always welcome."

"I wish it were a social visit, I've missed sitting and talking with you." He paused, "I've taken a small job, but some of it doesn't add up. It doesn't feel right."

"What kind of advice can an old fighter pilot give you?"

"Anything about the Last Will and Testament of Adolph Hitler?"

Bruno drained his glass and refilled it. He held out the bottle to Patrick who offered his glass for more. "Patrick, what are you involved in?" the old man asked cautiously.

Patrick took a long drink and launched into the story of his meeting with Walter King on the *Marienplatz.* He left nothing out. The old man listened attentively, silently, occasionally sipping from his glass. When Patrick finished the two sat in silence.

"A most amazing story, and the first time I have heard such a tale." Bruno walked to a book case and removed a folder. He returned and shuffled through the papers. "There were two documents, one was the shorter Will, and the other was the longer Political Testament. Hitler dictated both documents to his secretary, Traudl Junge, on 29 April 1945, the same day that he married Eva Braun. The executor for the Will was Martin Bormann. The Will was witnessed by Goebbels, Bormann and Colonel Nicholaus von Below."

He took another drink of brandy and adjusted his glasses before taking up the papers and continuing. "It's been suggested that the actual author of the Political Testament was Goebbels and that Hitler merely dictated from Goebbels's notes. The Testament was witnessed by Goebbels, Wilhelm Burgdorf, Bormann, and General Hans Krebs."

The old man set down the papers and shook his head. "Patrick, I have never heard of another Will, a second Will, nor heard any rumors or stories of a second Will. All the witnesses to the Testament died shortly afterwards. Berlin was a madhouse, a ravaged city. About your mysterious *SS* Major Strasser, again, I've seen no references to him. Many *SS* disappeared after the war, moved, changed names, records went missing or were destroyed. It was a bad time, a dark time." Bruno shook his head, "The *SS*, Patrick, they were a bad lot."

Patrick held out his glass, "Their uniforms were nice; some were made by Hugo Boss."

The old man scowled as he refilled Patrick's glass, "That's your mother talking. She spent the war drinking Absinthe and listening to Django play *Nuages* while she sketched frocks on tablecloths."

"And running guns to the *Macquis*," Patrick said.

Bruno shrugged, "I'm sorry I can't offer you any information on a second Will."

"Thank you, I suspected as much, but if anyone was to have heard of anything like a second Will I thought you might have knowledge of it."

Bruno considered for a moment. "Of course there are the legends surrounding Hitler's death; some saying he deliberately chose the date for Satanic reasons."

"Satanic?"

"*Walpurgisnacht*" Bruno smiled, "30 April to 1 May. Hitler committed suicide on the 30th of April."

Patrick nodded, remembering the *Walpurgisnacht* he and Heike attended in the Harz mountains, the annual celebration of the final victory of Spring over Winter, of the witch's celebrations and goblins. "Is that what you believe? That Hitler was in league with the devil?"

Bruno laughed, "I believe that it was more the advance of Zhukov and his Belorussian Army rather than the call of the supernatural. What, you think Hitler hiked through the Brenner Pass, took a *U-boat* to Paraguay or Argentina and is eating a *schnitzel* in South America now?"

"No," Patrick shook his head. "I think he died in the bunker. It was the Russians who had control of that area afterwards, so we may never really know. And he was a vegetarian."

Bruno laughed, clasped a bony hand on Patrick's shoulder and looked him in the eye. The old man knew better than to try to talk his friend out of the job. "Take care my boy, check your six, and trust your wingman."

As he said his goodbyes and walked away, Patrick considered the old man's advice. 'Check your six.' *Yes, I'll definitely watch my back. As for a trusted wingman, for now it looks like I'm flying solo.*

*****

The jolt of the train stirred him back to reality. It didn't make any sense. No one else had ever spoken of another Last Will and Testament. It was a fool's errand, but they were paying him 250,000 Euros to track it down. *OK, I can do that; a few days of leg work to check it out and I can close up the shop and spend a couple of weeks in Mallorca.* Still, that much money usually meant trouble.

Six

The Hamburg *Bahnhof* buzzed with the hustle and bustle of most large European city train stations, but Patrick easily navigated his way through the crowd to the front entrance. The day was gray and overcast, but not cold, so he didn't bother to put on his coat. He checked his watch and waited, enjoying being outdoors after hours in the train. His eyes picked up the blue BMW Z3 as it whipped around the corner; there was no mistaking the stunning brunette behind the wheel.

Hannelore pulled the car around and stopped in a free space a few meters away.

"It's a good thing I brought a small bag," he dropped his bag in the tiny trunk space.

"I didn't buy it for the trunk space, *Liebchen*."

They embraced with a kiss on each cheek. Hannelore beamed, "You look well. All is good, in *München*, with the business?"

"Yes, I'm well and the business is—OK."

Hannelore studied him for a moment. "You miss Heike. We all do. You still have a place in your heart for her, and *that* is why you are my favorite brother-in-law."

"Your *only* brother-in-law," Patrick laughed.

She smiled and blew him a kiss. The BMW roared to life as she dropped it in gear and pulled onto the *Amsinck Straße*. As she expertly guided the car through traffic, she reached in her purse for a cigarette. Patrick offered her a light.

"So you've taken a job?" She glanced at him, "I thought you were finished with that work, retired."

"It's 250,000 Euros, with 50,000 for a retainer and expenses. The shop only makes enough for me to keep it open."

"And you keep it open because…that's what Heike would have wanted?"

The silence between them confirmed Hannelore was correct.

"It's too much money, Patrick. That much money, dredging up old Nazi business, it can only spell danger and trouble. I'm worried for you." She quickly maneuvered between two trucks. "I called someone to help you, he will meet us tonight."

"I usually work alone, I've—"

"Dieter is a man, like you, with certain," Hannelore turned and smiled, "skills." She placed her hand on Patrick's leg, "Please, I'll feel better if you are not alone. *I* trust him."

Patrick settled back in the seat and relaxed, "Then I trust him as well." *I have a wingman.*

Seven

Berlin

Karl paced his living room, peering out his window at the street below for the second time in as many minutes. He was sure he had seen someone earlier. *Why had Otto been so impetuous? Why couldn't he have waited? Was it an accident, or had they killed him? Are they coming for me? And who are they and what do they want?*

   Karl was enjoying his modest pension after a long career as a mining engineer in the Harz Mountains when his old friend Otto tried to coax him out of retirement on some new adventure. *Damn fucking Otto!* Karl hadn't known exactly what Otto was looking for, poking around those old, cursed tunnels. Otto was excited, but elusive, saying only that he needed help in the tunnels. After the war, Karl helped the Allies map them out, and seal them up. He thought he was through with the *Obersalzberg* with all of its death and misery. *I'm too old to be dragged back into all of this.*

He walked to the desk and pulled out the Walther P-38 pistol, hefting the small automatic in his hand. *Fool's courage, I'm too old for any more battles.* He collapsed in a chair and poured himself another *Asbach*. It was a new bottle this morning—now it was nearly half empty. He downed the brandy and fell asleep in the chair.

The knocking at the door roused him from his fitful slumber. His back and neck were stiff; he ran a hand through his hair and rubbed his bleary eyes.

"*Herr* Kessler? *Herr* Kessler, I have a delivery, a package from Otto Schleiman."

"Leave it at the door…I…I just got out of the shower."

"*Herr* Kessler, you must sign for the package. I cannot leave it. My truck is outside. I must hurry to my next delivery."

Karl ran to the window and saw an ordinary delivery van outside.

"*Herr* Kessler?"

Karl crept to the door and looked through the security hole. He saw a man in a plain brown uniform holding a large padded envelope. Karl hefted the small pistol in his right hand, stepped back and opened the door.

He was too old, and they were professionals, too young and fast for him. Before Karl knew it the man in the brown uniform and two others, waiting on each side of the door, swept into the room, closed the door behind them and disarmed him. One of the men threw a vicious punch into his solar plexus causing Karl to double-up and crumble to his knees. Sufficiently softened up, the men dragged him to the kitchen and sat him in a straight-backed wooden chair. One of them produced a roll of duct tape, taping Karl to the chair. Another grabbed a wash cloth from the sink and shoved it into his mouth, keeping the damp cloth in place with another piece of duct tape. The men worked wordlessly and quickly.

With Karl sufficiently secured, the two men left the kitchen. One went to stand near the front door and the other began to ransack the apartment. Karl was left alone with a third man, the one who looked like an accountant, a man with a high forehead and round eye glasses. The third man went to the kitchen counter, pulled on a pair of latex gloves, opened the drawers and rummaged through the contents.

"I need to know, *Herr* Kessler, everything that Otto Schleiman told you." He picked up a tool used to core apples and held it until it glinted in the kitchen light. "Do not lie to me. You *will* tell me everything I want to know." The man spoke fluent German. "Tonight may be the last night of your life. I can make it go quickly or…"

The old clock in the living room chimed eight times. Karl Kessler never heard it chime nine.

Eight

Patrick and Hannelore descended the steps on the side of the Hamburg *Rathaus* and entered the *Ratsweinkeller.* Hannelore exchanged pleasant greetings with Rudi, who led them to a table in the corner, while Patrick studied the various wooden ship models suspended from the vaulted ceiling.

Hannelore eyed Patrick as she removed a dark cigarillo from its silver case and accepted the light offered by Patrick. "You've always liked this place, haven't you?"

"I have. It's got a lot of charm, and great food." He paused, "It was the first place Heike and I…"

"We had an agreement," Hannelore said, "not to see our clients on a personal basis. Outings to events and sex clubs were one thing, but a personal involvement… She broke our rule—for you." She crushed out her cigarillo. "She changed her life—for you."

"It wasn't exactly a one way thing, I-"

She placed her hand on his, "*Liebchen*, I understand; you both tried to create new lives, and for a while you succeeded. Heike was happy, she loved you. I was happy for both of you; I care about you, it's why I asked Dieter to go with you. He will join us after supper. Right now he and Mathias are cruising the *St. Pauli* district."

"Mathias is…?"

"His lover, his deck hand," Hannelore said simply. She looked at Patrick, "This does not bother you?"

Patrick smiled, "I first met you and Heike while chained to a cross in your dungeon, I'll make no judgments of others."

Hannelore lips turned into a wicked smile, "You were the most amazing client; I saw that Heike wanted you for her own."

The drinks came; Hannelore smiled and thanked the waiter.

Patrick picked up his beer and nodded his approval as he took his first taste. "Is Monika still performing at the Bamboo Club?"

Hannelore laughed. "Yes, she is doing a Snow White act that will forever change the way you think about Disney, Snow White never had battery operated devices!"

They both laughed.

"It's good to see you again Patrick, and it's good to see you laugh. But this business you are involved in, lost Nazi documents, thousands of Euros at stake, dead archeologists, it's no good, no good."

Patrick drank more beer. "I don't disagree, but sometimes…" He let the thought trail off and Hannelore didn't press the issue.

"I know you are capable *Liebchen*. Heike said you killed a man in Beirut and one in Dublin."

Patrick silently looked at her.

Hannelore nodded her head to one side and shrugged. "It bothers me not. Some people deserve to die. I believe you are a good man. I don't believe my sister could have fallen in love with someone who was not good."

Patrick nodded and looked away.

Hannelore reached out to touch his arm. "Please be careful *Liebchen*, protect yourself."

The rest of the meal was spent in innocent conversation, gossip, what various friends and acquaintances were up to, and ribald tales of Hannelore's clients, which had Patrick laughing. "Dressed as a, what do you call it? *Ach, Ja*, cheerleader, yes, cheerleader."

Dieter was waiting when they arrived at Hannelore's apartment. Hannelore and Dieter embraced and Dieter extended one of his large hands, swallowing Patrick's. Patrick was a stout six-foot, but felt small next to Dieter's imposing figure.

When Hannelore asked where Mathias was, Dieter's reply was curt. "He watches." Dieter's command of English was not up to that of Hannelore's but both she and Patrick understood. Mathias was out there, somewhere, watching the apartment, keeping an eye on things. Patrick gave Dieter a slight nod and smile of approval. This job was no less dangerous, but he felt better for the involvement of Dieter and Mathias.

The three of them relaxed in Hannelore's living room, the lights of Hamburg twinkling outside. Hannelore rang a bell and Katja quietly entered the room. Hannelore gave the girl everyone's drink order and dismissed her. As Katja left the room she eyed Dieter's muscled bulk.

Patrick pulled the paper from his pocket. For Dieter's benefit he spoke German. He explained about the archeologist who died in the tunnel looking for the location of Hitler's *true* Last Will and Testament, told them of his conversation with Walter King, and showed them the paper that King had given him. It contained the names, addresses and phone numbers of Otto Schleiman and Karl Kessler. Patrick asked Dieter if he could check out a car, giving him the information on the Audi that had picked up Walter King at the *Marienplatz*.

Dieter wrote it all down in a small notebook, put the notebook in his pocket and nodded. "There is a clerk at motor vehicles. He will be easy for Mathias."

Patrick held up a hand, "I don't want Mathias to do anything—"

"The clerk is young, and willing" Dieter said. "Mathias will do him, gladly. I do not worry. Mathias knows who is the Master."

Hannelore smiled a wicked smile, but Patrick let it go.

When Katja came and served the drinks, Hannelore gave her the phone number for Karl Kessler, telling her to call and see if he was in. Katja was to say that *Herr* Kessler had won a new vacuum cleaner, and while they all laughed, they agreed the idea was so bizarre it might actually work.

Patrick told what he knew about the real will, the last days of Hitler in the bunker, what Walter King had told him of Major Jürgen Strasser, and what he'd learned from Bruno Wenz. He finished as Katja returned.

The young girl bowed before her Mistress saying that *Herr* Kessler's phone had rung several times but was not answered. Hannelore dismissed her to prepare the guest bedroom for Patrick.

"He could be out, drinking, visiting friends," Patrick offered.

"Perhaps," Hannelore said, but there was something in her reply, that hint of woman's intuition that said she didn't necessarily believe it.

They finished their drinks and decided to call it a night. Dieter would come by tomorrow morning to accompany Patrick to Berlin to check on Karl Kessler. Mathias would stay in Hamburg and 'watch.'

Hannelore escorted Dieter to the door and Patrick excused himself to retire to the guest room.

He arrived at the finely furnished room, not surprised to find the nubile young Katja kneeling on the floor at the foot of the bed, holding a soft robe in her hands. She had unpacked his suitcase, and appeared to be waiting for him to shower and change. Patrick stripped and took a quick shower. When he emerged from the shower he donned the soft cotton robe and settled into the luxurious chair, leaning back and opening the robe.

Katja slinked across the floor with the feline grace of a predatory jungle cat, coming to rest between his legs. She pushed aside the folds of his robe, gently taking his manhood in her hands.

Patrick closed his eyes and allowed his head to fall back into the chair. He would gladly accept this gift, this generous show of hospitality from Katja. He realized both of them would find pleasure in it.

Katja possessed the hands of an angel; softly caressing his shaft, she leaned forward to gently kiss the head. Her tongue traced a moist line around its girth.

A soft moan emanated from Patrick's lips as he melted into the chair.

Katja continued her ministrations to his swelling cock, pumping it as she brought the head into her mouth. She slowly descended on its length, her warm, moist and tender mouth a cavern of delights.

Her lips held the tumescent shaft firmly, but gently, while her tongue flicked and danced around it. With softly probing fingers she cupped his balls, kneading them, tenderly stoking them with her fingernails. She felt him tense; he wouldn't last long.

Katja felt it coming as Patrick arched his back, gripping the arms of the chair in his last throes. When he erupted she swallowed, drinking it down, and licking away the vestiges.

She gently backed away, slowly easing the sated organ from her mouth. Her tongue continued to lick the shaft up and down, a final homage to his wondrous appendage. Wordlessly, she rose to fetch a warm washcloth to clean him.

Patrick remained in the chair, eyes closed, sublimely satisfied. He would sleep well tonight and begin the hunt tomorrow.

Katja finished her duties, quietly leaving the room, treading softly on her naked feet to Mistress's bedroom. A pleasure slave's work was never done, but it was nearly always satisfying.

Nine

The sleek lines of the massive white yacht stood out against the glass-like, azure water. The Grand Vizier was one of the jewels of the Mediterranean, a veritable floating palace, business center, and part-time home to one of the richest men in the Middle-East. Rumors abounded about the lavish and decadent lifestyle of the yacht's owner. Those fortunate enough to be invited aboard seldom talked about the owner or his parties. Curiosity seekers were dissuaded by the potent security force that guarded the vessel and its mysterious owner.

Ja'bar al-Zubair used the sliver of burning cedar to light the end of his Partagas cigar. He enjoyed the ritual, the smell of the rich Cuban tobacco, the glowing end of the fine, hand-rolled cigar. He preferred to believe the stories that they were rolled on the bare thighs of young Cuban girls. His fingers switched on a bank of security cameras and he studied the three blonde women sunning on the yacht's upper deck. He smoked as he watched them. While he would have them that evening he despised them, *Women who care for nothing but caviar, drinking and shopping*.

There was a knock at the door and Hakim, his trusted secretary, entered the room and bowed.

Hakim walked to the desk and presented the folder, "The Tokyo financials."

Zubair studied the long, even, gray ash, the sign of a quality hand-rolled cigar and nodded approvingly; he appreciated quality. He knocked the ash into an ashtray and accepted the folder, "Thank you, old friend. What of our European venture, the Germans?"

"The contact was made." Hakim gave a slight bow, "Deveraux accepted the assignment."

"Excellent! It goes well, perhaps we settle old scores."

"You believe King will double cross Deveraux?"

"I'm counting on it. King is an opportunist. He will bring us the document and remove Deveraux."

"And the death of your cousin, Hassan, will be avenged," Hakim added.

"Yes, I've not forgotten Deveraux's actions in Beirut. His involvement in this enterprise, and his hopeful demise, are a much appreciated extra. He escaped us once."

"And the document?"

"My dear Hakim, the recovery of the document is essential. It will be the cornerstone, the platform for a rebirth of the Aryan Supremacists and Neo Nazis, something to rally those who oppose the Zionists. This will become our distraction, our ruse, while everyone is focused on this new threat, our brothers in Jihad can work their plans." Zubair gave a laugh, "It *is* ironic, is it not?

The vaunted Patrick Deveraux, once a terrorist and IRA assassin himself, now dies to instill new terrorism."

Hakim smiled, "Create turmoil and dissension, incite new hatred for the Zionists, and in the process settle old debts. It is an excellent plan."

Zubair dismissed the thought with a wave of his hand. "It is a sideshow to the real struggle, but we do what we can."

Ten

Patrick and Dieter took the plane from Hamburg to Berlin and picked up the rental car that Katja arranged for them. Patrick would have preferred the train, not that he was afraid of flying, but he liked the relaxed atmosphere of train travel. Dieter liked trains, as his bulk did not comfortably fit most airline seats.

But this wasn't a pleasure trip, this was work, and they hoped to be back in Hamburg that evening. Dieter left the *Tempelhof* airport, driving north on the *Wilhemstrasse*. As they turned east on the *Unter den Linden*, Patrick cast a backwards look at the *Brandenburger Tor*, one of the architectural icons of Berlin. They drove through town, past the *Alexanderplatz* until they reached the residential area and the apartment of retired mining engineer Karl Kessler.

It was a modest neighborhood, in the throes of rebounding from years of neglect behind the Communist side of the wall. Dieter parked the car down the street and they walked to the third floor apartment of *Herr* Karl Kessler.

Dieter turned to watch the hallway while Patrick knocked on the door. He knocked three times, but got no answer. The two men exchanged glances.

He knocked again. "*Herr* Kessler?"

Patrick looked to Dieter who shrugged and looked away. Patrick pulled out his billfold, removed lock picks, and easily opened the door. Both men quickly slipped inside, closing the door behind them. Instantly they were on guard; the room was in shambles, it had been expertly tossed, and reeked with the coppery smell of human blood. They stood, silent for a moment and then efficiently inspected the remaining rooms. The bathroom and small bedroom were also in disarray, having been thoroughly searched. In the kitchen they found the body of Karl Kessler, taped to a chair, his blood pooled and congealed on the floor.

Dieter immediately began wiping down everything they had touched. They needed to see if they could find anything, and leave as if they'd never been there. "Professionals, if they found nothing, we find nothing."

"I agree," Patrick examined the body of the late Karl Kessler. He'd been brutally used and didn't go slowly. *What were they after? What did they think he knew?* He checked the phone to see if there had been any messages. The old man had no computer, no cell phone that he could find, but Kessler had died for something, even if he didn't know what it was. "Anything?"

"*Nein*," Dieter replied.

"So, who knew about Kessler's involvement in this, other than me?"

Dieter shrugged, he knew it was a rhetorical question.

"Walter King, for one; he was the one who gave me the information on where to find Karl Kessler. Why would King give me the information, and then look up Kessler himself and kill him, if that's what happened?"

Again Patrick got only a silent shrug from Dieter.

Patrick slowly turned to take in the carnage around him: the rooms and the grotesque corpse of Karl Kessler. "It all connects, somehow it all connects. We just don't know how—yet. Let's get back to Hamburg."

As they left Kessler's apartment building they saw the *Bundespost* truck driving away. They looked at each other, Dieter gave a 'why not?' shrug and went back to the building. He quickly returned, smiling and holding a small brown envelope postmarked Bavaria.

As they drove to the airport Patrick examined the envelope, turning it over in his hands. There was nothing particularly noteworthy; it was a standard stationary store padded envelope for mailing. It was addressed to Karl Kessler. The return address was "O.S." with a Stuttgart street address and it was postmarked last Thursday.

Timing is everything, Patrick mused. The *Bundespost* was usually quick and efficient. Normally this package, and its contents, would have been there, and Kessler's uninvited guests would have found it, but for some reason, the package was delayed. As Dieter drove down the *Unter den Linden*, Patrick held the unopened envelope in his hands and looked out the window. *They would have killed Kessler anyway, but he died without ever knowing 'why' it was all happening. What the fuck have I gotten myself into?*

Patrick opened the envelope while Dieter pulled over at an *Imbiss* for food. The envelope contained a hiking map of Berchtesgaden, a *'Wanderkarte,'* and another tourist map of the old Nazi tunnel system beneath the *Obersalzberg*. There were handwritten notes on both of the maps. When Dieter returned with two bratwursts and two beers, Patrick offered him the maps.

Dieter looked at the maps while he ate a brat, washing it down with a beer. "Schleiman?"

Patrick swallowed a bit of his own brat, "That'd be my guess."

Dieter looked at the maps and back again at Patrick. "We go to Bavaria?"

"The trail to *Herr* Kessler and Berlin was a dead end." Patrick chuckled at the pun, but Dieter remained impassive. "Yes, we go to Bavaria, but first we need to get back to Hamburg. I want to see what Mathias came up with and check on Hannelore."

While Dieter threw away the remains of their hasty lunch, Patrick tried to figure out exactly what to do next. He didn't really have a plan, and he needed one.

Eleven

Katja greeted them at the door and took them to Hannelore and Mathias in the living room while she went for drinks.

Hannelore rose to embrace both men, relieved to see them safely returned.

Mathias stood, politely, yet warmly, shaking Patrick's hand in greeting. Mathias was a modest five-seven, with an angelic face and dark, curly hair, set atop a lean, but well-muscled physique. He seemed almost cherubic, yet he'd been tested as a deck hand in the cruel North Sea, and Captain Dieter had never found him wanting for courage. Dieter took the young man in his arms and kissed him.

As Katja served the drinks, Patrick told Hannelore and Mathias about the trip to Berlin. He didn't spare any of the gory details concerning Kessler's death and Mathias and Hannelore didn't shrink from the gruesome narrative.

When he finished he paused, giving everyone a chance to consider the possibilities. No one spoke; and he turned to Mathias, "Anything on the car that picked up

Walter King after our meeting at the *Marienplatz*?"

Mathias set down his beer, taking a small notebook from his pocket. "I know someone at motor vehicles. We met for lunch. I, uh, I got this information. The car, the Audi at the *Marienplatz*, my friend ran the license number and it's registered to a Heinrich Schiff in Stuttgart. I have a name, address and picture," he handed the information to Patrick. "The business card that King gave you, the phone number leads to a message call center, where he, or someone, gets the message. It doesn't do us much good."

Patrick nodded; it was something he expected. Dieter merely grunted.

Patrick studied the photo of Heinrich Schiff for a moment. "I didn't get a good look at anyone except King, and this isn't him." The group was silent. "So we have nothing."

Hannelore lit a cigarillo and expelled a stream of smoke. "You have a dead body in Berlin and the maps that came in the mail."

All silently nodded in agreement as Patrick looked on. "Yea, OK. So, we'll shake the tree, beat the bushes."

Hannelore's eyes widened, "You're forcing them to make the next move?"

Patrick took a moment to consider the options. "Here's what we'll do. Dieter and I will head south to the *Obersalzberg* to check out the information on the maps we got from Kessler's apartment. On the way down we need to draw them out, force their hand. Mathias, you call the phone number on the business card, the one for the message center. You need to make King, or whoever gets the message, believe you know what happened at Kessler's apartment, and that money can buy your silence. Agree to meet them somewhere public, somewhere safe, somewhere like…" Patrick looked around for help.

Dieter swallowed a glass of *Schnapps*, and held it out to Mathias for a refill, "Rothenburg."

Patrick thought about it, "Yea, that would be good, always lots of tourists, alleys, shops, easy to disappear and mingle, very public. It's in northern Bavaria so we can easily get down to the *Obersalzberg*." He smiled at Dieter, "*Sehr gut!*"

Dieter returned the smile, toasting Patrick with a drink of *Schnapps.*

Patrick turned to Mathias. "Tell whoever you make contact with that you will meet them in front of the *Rathaus* in Rothenburg day after tomorrow at two p.m. Say you will be holding a guide book in your left hand and a red umbrella in your right."

Mathias wrote in his notebook.

Patrick went over more details, verifying cell phone numbers, code words, and possible rendezvous points. Satisfied that they had at least some kind of plan they enjoyed another round of drinks before Hannelore escorted Dieter and Mathias to the door to bade them good night.

Hannelore pulled Dieter to the side, "This has gotten dangerous, yes?"

"These men are killers," Dieter said, "what they did to the old man, Kessler…"

"Maybe you should call her," Hannelore looked back to the room with Patrick, "I'd feel better, if there were more of you, please?"

Dieter's eyes twinkled, "I will."

Hannelore returned to the living room to find

Patrick reclined in his chair, his eyes closed. She moved behind him, rubbing his shoulders. "You must relax *Liebchen*. This is dangerous work. You need to keep your wits about you. I wish you could leave this alone."

"You know I can't. Not at this point, not now. With Kessler dead I have to see this through, finish it. I don't want them coming back later after me…or you."

He stood and pulled Hannelore close to him. "Sorry to have dragged you into this."

They broke the embrace and Hannelore picked up a bell to summon Katja. As she shook the bell she turned to see Patrick staring at a leather cat-of-nine-tails on a nearby table.

Hannelore cautiously eyed him. "How long has it been?"

Patrick was silent, his eyes fixed on the wicked leather whip.

Hannelore moved beside him. "You need that, *Liebchen*. You and I both know it. But now is not the time, and *I* am not the one."

Patrick turned to face her.

"No, *Liebchen*. I know what you need, but I cannot give this to you. I won't take Heike's place. How long has it been? Have you seen anyone?"

"I don't know, maybe…two years?"

Hannelore gently touched his face. "Too long, much too long for someone like you; you need this badly. When this job is over you must see a friend of mine, *Die Gräfin*, she is in *München*. You know of her?"

Patrick nodded. *Die Gräfin, the Countess.*

Hannelore smiled. "I will call her, when this is finished, and she will help you. You trust me, yes?"

"Yes, I trust you. Thank you."

Hannelore turned to the door and summoned Katja, bending her over a chair. Hannelore picked up the cat and shook out the tails, the rustling of the leather the only sound in the room. She slowly drew the leather over Katja's naked bottom.

Patrick unconsciously backed up, providing room for the upcoming scene.

Hannelore grabbed the young girl's hair from behind and turned her face to her own. Her mouth came down on Katja's in a hard and savage kiss that was broken only when she pushed Katja's head back into position. She walked behind, eyeing the form bent over the chair. Turning, she smiled at Patrick, blew him a kiss, and began a slow and sensual massage with the leather tails.

Katja moaned and writhed under the lash, not from the pain, but from the erotic sensation. Even so, Hannelore stepped up her leather onslaught, increasing the speed, impact and ferocity. Katja continued to writhe and moan, now squealing as the harder blows wrought that delicious pain from deep inside her. Hannelore changed to an underhanded style, bringing the tails up from the bottom, the leather tips caressing Katja's exposed and tender sex. Katja shrieked, but never broke position.

Patrick was frozen in place, his eyes transfixed on the scene before him. He could feel Katja's pain and excitement. For a moment, more than a moment, he wanted to trade places with her. Hannelore was right; it had been too long.

With a flourish Hannelore finished Katja off, the last stinging blows bringing both women to the verge of climax. Dropping the whip at Katja's feet, Hannelore pulled the girl into a deep kiss. Their lips touched, Hannelore tasting the salty tears shed by Katja. Hannelore's tongue snaked into Katja's yielding mouth, parting the succulent, young lips. Katja caught her Mistress's tongue and lovingly sucked it. As they broke the kiss Hannelore gently wiped away Katja's tears, softly whispering "Go and wait for me." Hannelore turned to Patrick.

"Was that for my benefit?" he asked.

Hannelore smiled. "*Liebchen,* I do what I want for me, but if you enjoyed it as well... You wanted to trade places with her. It's understandable. We all have needs."

She placed a tender kiss on his cheek. "When this is over you must visit *Die Gräfin*. You need it. You know I am right. Yes?"

"Yes, thank you."

"Sleep well, *Liebchen*."

Patrick walked to his bedroom, the erotic image of Katja's flogging burned into his mind.

*****

The next day found Patrick and Dieter on a flight to Frankfurt where they picked up a black BMW for the drive south to Rothenburg. The drive would give them time to make sure they weren't being followed or watched and, if so, lose the offending parties. Utilizing a combination of country roads and the *Autobahn* they insured that they were indeed alone.

Late in the day they drove under the *Galgen Tor* and into the walled city of Rothenburg. *The Galgen Tor, the Gallows Gate* Patrick mused, *the gate that led to the gallows. Is that significant?*

Hitler's Will

Dieter checked them into a hotel just off the town square while Patrick went to call Mathias. They agreed to meet in the hotel's *Weinstube* in fifteen minutes.

Patrick walked around the corner and into the town center. As expected, it was full of tourists, including the usual bus loads of Japanese. Yes, they were in a walled city, closed in with untold places to disappear. If they were contained, well, so too were their antagonists, if they were here. Patrick made the call to Mathias, who picked up on the second ring. "You made the call?"

"Yes," Mathias said. "I left a message and they called back, very quickly. I think the message service thing is false, a...front?"

"Yea, not surprising, so…."

"They wanted more information. I told them nothing except that I knew what they did to Kessler and that they should meet me in Rothenburg tomorrow."

"Good. What about the phone?"

"In the Elbe, I bought a cheap phone and some minutes on a card and tossed it in the river after the call."

"OK." Patrick smiled, *Mathias has the face of an angel but the guile of a fox.* "Keep an eye on Hannelore and Katja. From what Walter King knew about me he probably knows about Hannelore as well. I doubt he'll move on them, but I want to be sure they're safe."

Without another word they ended the call. Patrick went to the *Weinstube* and sat with Dieter. A *Maibock* beer was already waiting for him.

"All is good, with Mathias?" Dieter asked.

"*Alles gut,*" Patrick sipped his beer.

Twelve

Mathias rose from the back seat of the car, and watched with bleary eyes as the van made its second pass around the block. His eyes never left it as it parked a few meters down from Hannelore's house. *Deliveries at five in the morning?* He watched as a man in a delivery uniform exited the van, and walked to the back of Hannelore's house; he carried a simple padded envelope. Mathias picked up his cell phone and dialed the number.

Katja woke instantly to the vibration under her pillow. Her hands quickly found the button to acknowledge the call, and she silently slipped out of bed and into the hallway.

Kurt paused for a moment at the back door of Hannelore's house. He waited, listening, and hearing no sounds, his practiced hands picked the lock and he slipped in. *No alarm system, stupid women.* He pulled his gun from the padded envelope and moved down the hall toward the stairs leading to the upstairs bedrooms.

Katja silently emerged from behind the door and

stood behind the man who was poised at the bottom of the stairs. "*Hallo*," her thick Czech accent broke the morning silence.

He turned quickly, leveling his gun at her. His eyes gleamed at the young woman before him; she was naked, her short red hair tousled. He noted the neatly trimmed patch between her legs, *a real redhead*. In her bare feet she was short, but she had the physique of a gymnast. Despite the early hour of the morning her green eyes were alive and her full lips split into a seductive smile.

She stood, silently, facing him. Kurt gave an upwards gesture with his gun, and Katja slowly raised her hands.

Kurt smiled, *King was right; one man is enough for this job.*

It was hard for him to comprehend what happened next. The girl exploded into the air in a flurry of hands and feet. He felt stabs of pain, his vision blurred; in seconds he crumpled, unconscious, to the floor.

*****

Patrick and Dieter met for breakfast in the hotel dining room. The morning *Frühstück* was appetizing and Dieter returned to the table with a plate full of sausages, meats, cheeses, breads and hard-boiled eggs.

Patrick's plate contained a few slices of cold cuts, cheese and a *Brötchen*. He looked at Dieter's plate. "Sorry about the fish."

Dieter grunted and continued eating. As a North Sea fisherman he would normally enjoy herring on his breakfast plate.

A young *Fräulein* came with coffee, smiling at them, especially Dieter. He smiled back, but he gave a better smile to the young man clearing plates from the tables.

Patrick sliced a *Brötchen*, buttering both pieces, making a sandwich with the cold cuts and cheese. "The meeting is at two this afternoon. We need to be in place by one. I want to check out the crowd, do a little recon."

Dieter managed to get out a "*Ja*" between mouthfuls. "This morning I see someone, take care of some things."

The most effective disguises are usually simple and low key, requiring only subtle changes. People see what they expect to see, so a slight bit of camouflage is often all that is required. Patrick wore baggy pants, a coat that was a bit too large, and parted his hair in the middle. He added large rectangular glasses, a hat, and carried a battered, brown briefcase. When he looked at his reflection in the mirror what he saw looked like a slightly disheveled professor. He doubted that Walter King would be able to pick him out of the crowd in the marketplace. Feeling safe and unassuming in the crowd, he went to mingle in the town center.

Thirteen

Kurt slowly returned to consciousness. He tried to move but found he was restrained. As he awoke he realized he was naked, and tied to a leather spanking horse. Heavy leather cuffs and chains stretched his limbs, holding him tight. The room was dark and windowless. A voice from the corner startled him.

"Why are you here? Why do you come into my home?"

He was silent.

Footsteps advanced; the lights suddenly came on, momentarily blinding him. As his eyes adjusted to the light he saw his captors. A young man with curly hair stood next to a tall, stunning brunette, *Hannelore, the one I was supposed to take.*

Kurt watched as Mathias and Hannelore went through his belongings: his wallet, some Euros, a cell phone, a set of keys, and a multi-tool.

Hannelore gave it all a cursory look, and turned to Mathias, "Check out the van, see what you can find. Then move it off the street, dump it in an underground parking garage and leave it, then get back here. Katja and I will attend to our uninvited visitor. As soon as we have some information we'll contact Patrick and Dieter." She turned and gestured to Katja, who stood across the room, next to a heavy punching bag.

Kurt stared at the young woman who had exploded before him the last time they'd met.

"People are only useful to me if they do many things. Katja is pretty, a good cook, and is wonderful in bed." Hannelore snapped her fingers and Katja exploded again, delivering a flurry of kicks and punches that had the heavy bag shaking on its chains. "She is a very effective bodyguard. Now, who are you? Why are you here? Who is Walter King? What does he want? Where is he? What happened to Karl Kessler?"

The room was silent.

Hannelore grabbed a handful of Kurt's hair in her fist, "You *are* going to answer these questions. You WILL tell me what I want to know."

"FUCKING BITCHES!" Kurt screamed.

Katja's eyes went wide, and her mouth opened in abject horror. Even Mathias gasped and backed up a step.

Hannelore cruelly jerked Kurt's head around, "Observe your situation."

The floor beneath him was covered with a heavy plastic tarp. Across the room he saw a cleaning bucket and bottles of chlorine bleach. Kurt looked at his three captors. None were hiding their faces. They didn't care if he could identify them because… He spat on the floor at Hannelore's feet, "Fuck you!"

Hannelore backhanded Kurt, bloodying his nose

and ripping her latex glove on one of his teeth. She ripped off the glove and pulled another over her hand. "Give me the cane. I think we'll skip the warm up with this one."

Mathias handed Hannelore the thin rattan cane. She took the savage reed from his hand and nodded to the door, Mathias's sign to leave. He didn't envy the intruder his fate.

Katja slinked across the room, a feral smile on her lips. For the first time the man was afraid.

There were no clocks in Hannelore's dungeon. Time did not exist for her clients, nor did it exist now, for her prisoner. It had been over two hours, and her guest was nearly used up. Hannelore herself was tired; she normally paced herself better. Typically she didn't let her emotions get the better of her, but she was angry at this man, the man who invaded her house, intending to harm her and Katja.

Hannelore and Katja rested in another room, making their victim wait in silence for his torment to begin again.

Katja handed Hannelore a bottle of water. "*Herrin* Helga says that torture is the quickest way to a lie; that they will say anything to make it stop."

Hannelore smiled at the mention of her stunning blonde protege, Lady Helga. "Helga would be correct. Even strong men, clever men, such as Patrick and Dieter will lie—and eventually break. Everyone has a breaking point; there comes a time when the lies are used up, and all one has left is the truth." She glanced to the floor, where their prisoner waited in the dungeon below. "This one, he is not so strong and clever."

When Mathias returned from his errand his eyes

recoiled in horror at the figure restrained over the spanking horse. True to her word Hannelore didn't have a warm-up. There'd been no gentle and sensual flogging to stimulate and awaken the nerve endings, nothing to get the endorphins going. She'd brutally used the cane and attacked the man, quickly leaving welts and drawing blood.

Things she never did with a client, even if they begged for it, she did to him. For the first hour she asked no questions, she simply gagged him and beat him unmercifully, softening him up. To make it easier for Mathias to handle him later, she viciously caned the soles of his feet and the palms of his hands. "If he can't stand, or can't hold on to anything, he'll be easy to manage."

After her initial assault she removed the gag and started questioning him. He tried to hold out, but she could read men in these situations, and she saw him beginning to crack. If her prisoner thought he was due a respite he was wrong.

Katja held a bottle under his nose and he recoiled at the strong vinegar smell. She moved behind him and tipped the bottle, letting the vinegar seep into the bloody cuts from Hannelore's cane. Kurt screamed, flailing against the restraints.

Hannelore continued her interrogation. "Why did you come into my home?"

Kurt merely grunted. Hannelore nodded to Katja who poured more vinegar into the wounds. He screamed again.

"Why did you come into my home?"

"In…ins…insurance…make sure Dev'ro did …the job."

Hitler's Will

Hannelore nodded to Katja, who laid another dozen hard and vicious strokes with the braided whip across Kurt's back. When she finished, the whip dripped with blood.

Hannelore took the whip and walked to her prisoner. She whipped Kurt's cock and balls, bringing the wicked leather tails up from below, flicking her wrist, making Kurt thrash and shriek on the horse.

He was close to breaking. "What…what…do you…want?"

"I want you to tell me what I want to know. And you will."

Hannelore turned to Mathias. "Get the boat ready for a short trip. Come back later and pick him up. Katja and I will know everything we need to by then."

The man's screams echoed in Mathias's head even after he shut the door behind him.

Hannelore took another drink of water and watched as Katja's muscled arms delivered vicious blows with a wooden paddle. Their prisoner remained bound over the horse, his muscles and joints now in agony as was the rest of his body. She held up her hand, signaling Katja to stop. The room fell into silence for fifteen minutes.

Hannelore moved her chair closer to the beaten man. "We begin again."

Kurt groaned "No…no..."

"Tell me, who is Walter King?" Hannelore didn't wait for an answer but nodded to Katja who laid a savage cane stroke across the swollen and bloody buttocks.

Kurt screamed and strained against his bonds. "Aaaagggghhh!"

"Who is Walter King?"

"König… Not King…is Walther König."

"Where is he?"

"Don't—don't—know. South—*München*? Berchtesgaden?"

"What is he looking for? What does he want?"

"Papers—old—war documents. Nazi stuff."

"Why? Who does he work for?"

"Don't know. Big money—from—Arabs."

"Arabs? König works for Arabs?"

"For anyone… For money. Now—Arabs."

"Why?"

"Don't know... We just—do jobs."

"Your job today? Here?"

"Hold you. Make sure Dev…raux."

"Kessler, why was he killed?"

"Map… Thought—he knew—knew…"

"Where can we find Walther König?"

"Lives… Mannheim…don't…"

"How many men does König have with him now?"

"Uh—he—uh… Men…"

Hannelore slapped him hard across the face. "HOW MANY MEN?"

"Five—five… Is König and… Four."

She realized he was fading. They weren't likely to get much more useful information. She gestured to Katja who shut off the tape recorder. "Be ready to pack him up when Mathias gets back. Then clean up in here. I'm going to call Patrick, then shower."

Fourteen

Patrick mixed with the crowd, holding the guide book and umbrella as arranged, yet still completely aware of his environment, grateful that Dieter was out there somewhere, also watching.

As might a tourist, he positioned himself high on the *Rathaus* steps, providing security for his back, and giving him a good field of vision over the market place. As the clock neared two, the typical crowds gathered.

His practiced eye quickly found his target. It wasn't Walter King, but it was certainly who he was supposed to meet. *Is King here, watching?* He spotted Dieter, the big fisherman's towering height and blond hair making him stand out like a lighthouse beacon. Patrick continued to play the mark, while the contact worked his way through the crowd.

The man approached, taking careful note of the red umbrella and the tourist book. His eyes met Patrick's, silent confirmation of who they were to each other. The stranger extended a hand, pointing to a small café across the square. He spoke German, "Perhaps a coffee? We could talk?"

Patrick feigned uneasiness and nervousness, *let him think he has the upper hand, overconfidence may be his weakness.* "Yes, I, uh, that is acceptable." Patrick allowed the man to lead him to the café across the square, knowing Dieter would follow at a safe distance, watching to see if their visitor came with any handlers.

They sat at a table and ordered coffee. The stranger smiled and nodded to a case of pastries, large round balls of chocolate and powdered sugar, "Have you tried one of the *Schneeballen*? They're a local specialty."

"*Nein.*" Although it was always dangerous to assume anything, Patrick felt since the stranger was speaking German he didn't know he was Patrick Deveraux.

The coffees came, and they drank their coffee; each silently sizing up the other.

Outside the café, in order to blend with the tourists, Dieter purchased a cheap, disposable camera and was gesturing at a Japanese tourist to take a picture of him. It was a bit ludicrous, but Patrick felt better knowing that Dieter was watching his back.

The stranger spoke first. "You have information? Something you want to discuss?"

Patrick adopted his 'nervous professor' guise. "*Herr* Kessler, why was he killed?"

The stranger's face remained impassive. "What makes you think we had anything to do with the death of this man you call…*Herr* Kessler?"

"I—I saw something, that day, people, things." Patrick was purposefully being vague. Both men needed to get information in this exchange without offering any.

"I saw what you did." Patrick described enough of the carnage in Kessler's kitchen to add veracity to his story.

The man's eyes shifted, side to side, he was thinking, computing, figuring out the next thing to say, or do. He wasn't sure who Patrick was, but he was certain this crumpled professor had information, and he needed to know what he knew. "Perhaps, *Mein Herr*, we should talk somewhere more private. My hotel is not far from here. It is private, and safe."

Patrick looked around the restaurant as if he were scared or nervous. In actuality he was taking a quick inventory of everyone, to see if anyone followed them out. Clutching his briefcase, umbrella and tour guide close to his chest Patrick haltingly said "I, suppose so, if it is safe."

"Of course *Mein Herr*, perfectly safe."

As they exited the café Patrick noticed the woman at the pastry counter. She was blonde, stunningly attractive, wearing an exquisite, long camel hair coat and black leather boots. In her boots she was taller than he was.

They walked across the town square. The man led Patrick toward a row of buildings housing hotels, restaurants, and shops, but before getting to the hotel the man turned into an alley. Patrick followed, hoping that Dieter was watching his back. Despite the large amount of tourists in the town the alley was deserted. It was flanked by buildings and doors leading to various back doors, kitchens, and delivery entrances. The far end of the alley opened on to yet another street.

The light faded as they entered the brick canyon, the hustle and bustle of the market square receded into a murmur of ambient noise. Patrick had been in his share of dangerous alleys and streets and his senses were on high alert. He caught the scent of bread, vanilla and coconut as they passed an exhaust fan. His eyes continually scanned his surroundings and watched the hands and body movements of the man walking ahead. With each step he plotted a new defensive position.

Suddenly, halfway down the alley, Patrick saw a gray Mercedes pull across the far alley entrance. He couldn't see the driver, but when the rear passenger door opened he saw Walter King, sitting in the back seat, aiming a gun at him.

Everything seemed to happen in slow motion. Patrick saw his escort start to move to the side, out of the line of fire. Patrick instinctively moved to put the man between the shooter and himself. At the same time he threw his briefcase at the man, hoping to buy a second's distraction so he could move in for the kill. He heard a voice from behind him yell, "Patrick, DOWN!"

Patrick dropped to the ground, as two muffled gunshots flew over his head. He looked up the alley to see King close the door of the gray Mercedes as it sped away. The other man slumped against a wall, blood trickling down the front of his shirt. Patrick heard footsteps, and turned to see the tall woman in the brown coat and black boots, the woman he'd seen at the pastry counter. She walked past Patrick, an automatic pistol at her side, her heeled boots clicking on the cobblestones, straight towards the dead man,

Patrick jumped to his feet, still unsure about what had happened.

Behind him a black BMW pulled into the alley and stopped. Dieter stepped out and opened the trunk.

The mystery woman bent over the dead man,

opened his shirt, reached in and pulled out a microphone and transmitter. She turned, offering the device to Patrick, "He was wired, they were listening to you."

Patrick gazed at the wire and the dead man. "Who are…"

The woman reached in her pocket and held up a badge, Steffi Falke, *Nürnberg Polizei*.

Patrick looked at the badge, and back to the woman. *Steffi Falke? Police? Falke?*

Dieter ran forward, the woman rising to embrace him.

Realization flooded Patrick's face as the sibling resemblance came into focus. "Your sister? Your sister?"

Dieter nodded, "*Ja*, she comes to help. Better if they don't know I am with you, gives us advantage."

"*Scheiße*! Shit!"

Both men turned to look at the cursing Steffi, staring in horror at a blood stain on her exquisite coat. She turned to the dead man, raised her gun and pumped another round into his chest.

Patrick, no stranger to death and killing, watched in stunned horror. "He's already fucking dead!"

Dieter looked to Steffi, then at Patrick. "It was her favorite coat."

Patrick rolled his eyes, "I'll buy her another damned coat."

There was a moment of silence, then, for the first time, Steffi smiled. "*Danke*, Burberry, *bitte*."

Dieter carried the body to the trunk.

Patrick shook his head. *What the fuck have I gotten myself into?* His phone rang, it was Hannelore.

Fifteen

While Dieter and Steffi cleaned up the debris from the alley, Patrick took the call from Hannelore. He was impressed at the way they efficiently and professionally sanitized the 'crime scene'. Obviously there was more to Dieter than being the captain of a fishing boat, but he respected, and trusted Dieter, because Hannelore did.

Patrick listened as Hannelore briefly related the events of the break-in, and her interrogation of the intruder. "Everyone's OK?"

"Yes, everyone is safe, no one is hurt."

"They underestimated you," Patrick said. "They won't make that mistake again. You need to be even more careful. What about your uninvited guest?"

"Mathias takes him for a one-way cruise tonight."

"Is there anything else you can get out of him?"

Hannelore chuckled. "*Liebchen*, he is empty, used up, trust me, I know. He said there were five of them, König and four others."

"Three, now, we have one dead here."

"You killed him?"

"No."

"Dieter?"

"No, it was Dieter's sister. She showed up, out of nowhere, dropped the son-of-a-bitch dead in the alley, and scared off König, saved my ass." Patrick didn't know how he knew, but he could 'feel' Hannelore smiling at the other end of the phone.

"*Ach, Ja*, Steffi. I once offered her a job, to work with me. She is talented, a natural domme, would've made good money."

Patrick thought of the cool, beautiful blond who coldly walked by him, the automatic in her hand, striding straight for the dead man; the woman who didn't crack a smile until after she had put another round in the thug for bleeding on her coat. "Yea," he said, "I imagine she could."

"It was smart of Dieter to use Steffi. They still don't know about him, it gives you an advantage."

"Yea," Patrick agreed, "that's what he said."

"The man we have here, Mathias couldn't find anything of use on him, or in the delivery van."

"Doesn't surprise me, they're professional enough not to carry ID, probably using a safe house somewhere; but they've made mistakes. They've lost two of their own. They're bound to be more careful now."

He was interrupted by Dieter, "Patrick, we must go."

"Hannelore, we need to leave. I'll call later to see if you have anything new. Be careful, these men are dangerous. They won't make the same mistakes twice."

"You also *Liebchen*, be careful." The line went dead.

Steffi and Dieter embraced, and Steffi got in the black BMW. She smiled, nodded to Patrick, and drove off.

Dieter turned to Patrick. "I checked us out of the hotel. I have another car. We go?"

Patrick nodded, "Yes, to Berchtesgaden."

*****

Walther König sat in the back seat of the Mercedes as it sped along the *Autobahn*. He cursed under his breath. *Everything is going wrong, horribly, fucking wrong!* Things were spiraling out of control, and somehow he had to get it back together.

It was hours since he'd heard from Kurt. His last phone call said that there was no activity at the house in Hamburg, and he was going in to take the women. That was hours ago; Kurt hadn't called since, and was not answering his phone. Now he'd lost Horst in the alley, to some strange woman!

He was sure that the disheveled professor in the alley with Horst had been Patrick Deveraux, didn't the woman yell 'Patrick, down?' But why the disguise? The voice that he heard on the wire was not the voice that called to set up the meeting. That voice had been a much younger male.

Had Deveraux gone solo, was he trying to get the will, and shut them out? Only he, Walther König, knew who the customer was; who was paying them for this decades-old treasure.

König chuckled. Part of him, like Deveraux, doubted the very existence of this lost document. But if some be-robed, oil Sheik was giving him a million dollars now, and another million on delivery, he was damned sure going to come up with a lost Nazi document.

It was best now to regroup. He told Heinrich to drive to Berchtesgaden, picked up his cell, called Peter, and told him where to meet them. Lastly, he placed a call to the Stuber brothers. He disliked bringing in more people, that meant more payroll and less profit, but he had to find out what happened to Kurt in Hamburg.

His original five-man team was down to three, he'd been forced to recruit more help, and he was losing the initiative. An old saying crept into his thoughts: *The first one to make a mistake starts burying bodies.*

*****

The drive south from Rothenburg was quiet and uneventful. Neither Patrick nor Dieter spoke much. They bypassed *München,* deciding to spend the night somewhere quiet, off the beaten path, and arrive at Berchtesgaden the next day.

It was early in the evening when Dieter pulled the BMW off the *Autobahn* and drove a few miles to a local *Gästehaus*. He and Patrick had no reason to believe they were being followed, but the winding two-lane road to the small village provided ample opportunity to look for anyone watching them. Over beers, *Schnitzel* and *Spätzle* they tried to make sense of what had happened.

Patrick took a drink and looked at Dieter. "Calling your sister, Steffi, it was a good idea. She saved my ass."

Dieter nodded in acknowledgement. "I would be there, but better they think you work alone, or with a woman. It's best we travel by car now, we need to be armed, airports and train stations, not so good for that."

Patrick agreed, "Hannelore said that there were five of them."

"Three—now," Dieter replied. "Hannelore said they'd get rid of the other?"

"Yea, Mathias and Katja are taking him out on the boat. I imagine they'll be getting back soon."

"Mathias can handle the boat, for short trip."

"How long have you known Mathias?"

Dieter paused between mouthfuls of *Spätzle*. "Three years, since he is nineteen, I met him in Bremerhaven club, took him on boat as mate."

Patrick laughed, the pun obviously lost on the nearly always serious Dieter. "How long have you known Hannelore?"

Dieter paused, "A long time, before you met Heike, since when she and Heike were the most famous Domme sister pair in Hamburg, in Europe."

Patrick hesitated, "Did you…You, ever…"

The taciturn Dieter smiled. "Not my thing, but I knew them, they were big part of Hamburg scene, all the players knew them. I help them—sometimes." He stared at the table, "Heike…was special."

Patrick looked away. "Yes, special."

Dieter wasn't the kind to bond, hug, or console, at least not in public, but his voice softened, "With you, she was happy, she found what she wanted."

Patrick nodded, "Me too, I was happy."

They both realized the need to steer the conversation from the maudlin direction it had taken.

"I've read your dossier," Dieter leaned back in his

chair. "Your exploits, if true, make for interesting reading."

"*My* dossier?" Patrick turned his beer glass around and slowly wiped the beads of condensation from the logo. "And where did—"

"GSG-9."

"Ah," Patrick's Irish eyes came alive, "that explains a lot." He held up his glass, "To Special Operations."

"To Irish rogues," Dieter held up his own glass.

Patrick took another bite of *Schnitzel*, "Hannelore wasn't able to get much from her intruder, but we know this much: König hired me to get this supposed second Will and Testament and pay me 250,000 Euros for the job; his operation may be funded by Arabs; he's hired four others to help him; he visited Kessler ahead of us to try to find it; he tried to take Hannelore hostage to make sure I kept my end of the bargain if I got the papers; and he tried to kill someone, me, when he thought that person knew something about all of it."

Dieter took a long drink of his beer and held up the empty glass to signify he wanted another, "Dangerous people."

"They're good," Patrick agreed, "but not so good that they haven't made mistakes and lost two of their own."

Dieter received his second beer, took a drink, and smiled. "We are better."

Patrick smiled, raising his glass in a toast. "We are better."

Sixteen

It was nearly midnight when Mathias returned to Hannelore's. Katja met him at the door, and escorted him to the dungeon where he found the crumpled form of Kurt Rothe lying on a plastic tarp.

Hannelore was waiting in the dungeon. "Wrap him up and get him out of here, take him on his little cruise."

Dropping to the floor, Mathias began rolling up the body in the plastic tarp. As he pushed the body the near-lifeless form groaned. Mathias backed away, "He's not dead!"

Hannelore's icy look chilled him, and he went back to rolling up the body in the plastic tarp, securing it with heavy filament tape. Katja rolled in a two-wheeled dolly to help him get the body outside to the car.

The 'package' groaned again as he and Katja dropped it in the trunk. They secured the car and went back in the house.

Hannelore's instructions were terse. "Take Katja

with you, run up the Elbe somewhere, dump the body, and get back here."

Katja wasn't exactly Mathias's idea of a deck hand but he didn't doubt the girl's toughness, not any more. The two of them could handle the boat on this short trip, and he wasn't about to argue with either Hannelore or Katja. He knew that Dieter would want him to follow Hannelore's instructions. Mathias simply nodded, and he and Katja left.

The Stuber brothers watched the house from their Volkswagen Passat parked at the corner. Through the night vision goggles Katja and Mathias appeared as green ghosts as they carried something to the car and placed it in the trunk. Max dropped the goggles in his lap. "They put something in the trunk, think it was Kurt?"

"Maybe." Anton was the taller and smarter of the Stuber brothers. The reason they worked as a pair was that most people wouldn't hire Max alone. Max was tough enough; a good street fighter, but he lacked the intelligence and sophistication of his taller and younger brother. Anton fingered the pack of cigarettes in his pocket. He wanted a smoke, but was too professional to give away their surveillance for the sake of a glowing butt.

Max fidgeted. "Let's go in, check it out."

Anton looked at his watch; "We don't know who's in there, how many, or where they are. It's nearly midnight, and there's still activity. It's too risky right now. We stay, we watch, and if they leave we follow them."

"What did König say?" Max asked.

Hitler's Will

"He said to find out what happened to Kurt, that he'd gone into this house early this morning to hold the people inside for insurance against a job he was doing, and that he hasn't been heard from since. If Kurt's been taken we need know, and we need to find out what he's told them. Then we need to contain the situation."

"So?"

Anton turned to his brother. "So, if there are still people coming and going over twelve hours later I'm guessing that König's man Kurt fucked up. By doing so he's spoiled our element of surprise."

Max grunted, "You don't trust our friend, König."

"I don't trust anyone. König is an opportunist. He doesn't trust us; he's only told us the minimum we need to know."

There was movement at the end of the street, and once more Max brought the goggles to his eyes. "Those two kids, they're getting in the car."

Anton started the car and pulled out behind Mathias and Katja, maintaining a safe distance.

Max turned to look as they passed Hannelore's house. "What about the house?"

Anton slowly shook his head, "It will be there when we get back. Let's see where these two are going, and what they have in the trunk."

Anton was better at following someone than Mathias was at picking up a tail. The brothers easily followed as they drove towards the docks and *Der Norde Stern*. As expected, traffic was light during these early morning hours.

Max watched the street signs go by. "They're heading toward the docks, the river. What are they doing?"

Anton grimaced; Max didn't have the patience needed to be really good at this work. "That's why we follow them, to find out."

As they entered a long line of warehouses Anton dropped further back, the docks providing little traffic to hide behind. He saw the car ahead pass an open warehouse door, but as he neared the door a truck suddenly backed out of the open doorway and into the line of traffic. Anton braked hard, and sounded his horn. The startled truck driver slammed on his brakes, effectively blocking traffic. All Anton could see were the taillights of Mathias's car fading into the distance.

Max got out of the car, and began yelling at the hapless truck driver. Through exchanged curses and gestures the truck driver got his rig started, and cleared out of the way.

With precious minutes lost Max returned to the car, and they drove down the line of warehouses. Anton looked at his brother, "Relax, I'm betting this is a one-way road; they'll be waiting at the end. In fact, this may be the perfect place to meet our new friends."

When they reached the end of the road they were, indeed, at the waterfront. Parked by a warehouse was the car they had been following. A small fishing trawler was leaving the dock, making its way into the Elbe. Anton grabbed the night vision goggles, sighted the boat, and watched the ghostly, green images of Mathias and Katja come into focus. He dropped the goggles in Max's lap, and reached for a cigarette. "They'll be back, we'll wait." He reclined his seat, and lit a cigarette. "Let me know when the boat returns."

Seventeen

It was an uneventful trip; traffic on the Elbe was light, and Mathias easily found a deserted area to weight and dump the body. As he secured the chains and weights he felt the body move and heard a groan. He looked to Katja, who coldly returned his gaze. Her stern and impassive face told him he needed to continue, so he wrapped the last few chains, locking them to the concrete blocks. Katja helped him lift the package over the gunwale. With only a small splash, and a few bubbles, it slipped into the blackness of the Elbe.

Mathias piloted the boat back up the river, giving the larger craft a wide berth. Katja sat behind him watching the shoreline, as the lights passed by. The trip back was a silent one, their only conversations having to do with items related to the handling of *Der Norde Stern*. Although both had been in the alternative lifestyle for some time, and were rarely shocked by things, tonight was the first time either had been involved with something like this: murder.

Mathias turned to look at Katja. She seemed quiet, at peace. Even he didn't feel stressed by the recent events. A man was dead, that was true, and they were part of it, but the man brought this on himself. Katja trusted Hannelore, he trusted Dieter, and they believed this needed to be done. Perhaps later the enormity of what had transpired in the last few hours would affect them, but for now, they seemed coldly detached, performing the tasks needed to take care of business. They'd completed their mission, job done. Mathias cut back on the throttle, slowing the boat.

Katja felt the change and looked up.

"We'll be tying up soon," he said.

Katja nodded, zipped up her windbreaker, and joined Mathias in the pilot house.

They looked at each other in silence. The long day showed in their faces; they were both tired, and ready to bring this to a close.

"It's not our fault," Katja said. "The man made bad choices, bad decisions."

A silent nod was Mathias's only reply. He pointed to a group of lights and steered the boat in that direction, "Over there."

Katja dropped to the deck, to stand by the line.

Mathias noted her cat-like athleticism. Funny, he'd never noticed it before, now he saw it in her every move. He chuckled, *I never notice much about women at all.*

Mathias brought the boat into the berth, Katja jumping to the dock and holding the line. He shut down the boat as Katja secured the line. They barely turned to walk away from the boat when two men emerged from the shadows.

"Short trip, I don't see any fish," Anton said.

Max leered at Katja. "We'd like to look on your boat."

Katja subtly shifted into a semi-defensive stance, her legs slightly apart, the weight evenly distributed so she could kick with either foot. She sized up her opponents, who was closest, who looked more dangerous, more capable? Both men were more threatening than the intruder she had subdued yesterday morning. Katja guessed they were armed, but didn't see any weapons. She and Mathias were trapped, the boat and the River Elbe at their back, their only line of escape cut off by the Stuber brothers.

"We…We were testing an engine repair, when traffic on the river was light," Mathias said. The nervousness in his voice was evident, he was a bad liar.

Katja glanced at Mathias; saw the worry on his face. His courage and toughness as a seaman and deck hand were not in doubt, but he had no skills in hand-to-hand combat with professionals.

Anton took a step forward, "We're looking for our friend Kurt."

Mathias shrugged, "We, we don't know him."

Katja assessed her environment, looking for escape routes, cover, potential weapons, anything she could use. All the lessons and drills by Saburo, her Sensei, went through her mind.

"Maybe we'll look on the boat," Anton approached Mathias.

Mathias backed up, "No, the Captain wouldn't want us to—"

The taller Stuber brother stepped closer, quickly drawing a Taser from his belt.

Mathias threw a punch but was too slow. Anton had his Taser out, easily dodged Mathias's clumsy punch, and caught him in the ribcage with the Taser. The shock stopped Mathias where he stood, and he convulsed, falling backwards off the dock. He bounced off the *Norde Stern*, and fell into the black waters of the Elbe.

Max reached for his Taser, but Katja was quicker, lashing out with a vicious roundhouse kick to his side. As she brought her leg back she dropped to the ground, executing a leg sweep, knocking Max off his feet.

Katja turned to face Anton as she heard the splash. She didn't see Mathias, and cried out for him, "Mathias!"

Max was back on his feet, his Taser in hand. Both men advanced on Katja. She feinted a kick to the tall man, and quickly turned, landing a spinning back fist to Max's face. It was her last move. A stunning Taser shot from Anton, and then a second from Max dropped her to the dock. She heard ethereal voices say, "Check the boat, quick," before the darkness enveloped her.

Eighteen

Mathias was disoriented, his mind fogged as he slipped under the dark water. He couldn't remember when he'd felt such pain. Fortunately the cold, black water of the Elbe brought him to his senses. The will to live drove him to the surface, but he found the pain in his shoulder made using his left arm impossible. With his good arm he pushed his way to the surface, taking a breath of air.

He surfaced thirty feet aft of the *Norde Stern*, and waited and watched as the two men who attacked them searched the boat. Silently, he swam and hid behind near-by pilings. The men were talking, but he couldn't hear what they were saying. He looked and listened, but didn't see or hear Katja. Mathias felt he should do something, but what? *Where's Katja? Does she need my help?*

One of the men went to the stern of the boat, playing a flashlight over the water, obviously looking for him. Mathias pulled his head behind the piling. When he looked again he saw them leaving the boat, climbing onto the dock.

Moving to his right Mathias found an old wooden ladder. With one hand he gingerly climbed the ladder and peered over the edge of the dock. He saw the two men fold Katja's legs into the trunk and close the lid. As they got in the car Mathias pulled himself onto the dock. He strained to get a good look at the car and license plate. He kept repeating the license number, burning it into his brain like a sacred mantra. *The license number may be our only hope of saving Katja.*

As the car drove away Mathias collapsed on the dock, trying to catch his breath and recover from the assault to his body and senses. When the adrenalin rush subsided, and his chilled body started to shake, he rose to his feet and staggered to the boat. The two men had been quick, yet thorough, in their search of the boat. Things were tossed everywhere, it was a mess. *Dieter will kill them, just for that.* He found a paper and pen and wrote down the car information he'd been repeating to himself. He'd lost his cell phone when he fell in the water, but he knew he had to get back to Hannelore, she'd know what to do next.

Back on the dock he went to the car, and realized he didn't have the keys, he'd given them to Katja before they'd tied up at the dock. Cold, wet, and distraught over the abduction of Katja, Mathias walked, looking for some-one with a phone or a car.

Finally he stood at Hannelore's door, *why has it taken so long? How can I face her, tell her what happened?* He knocked on the door, and then again. Hannelore opened it to find Mathias, tears running down his face. "They have Katja," he sobbed.

Nineteen

Katja heard the voices before she saw anything. Some-where she heard people talking, shouting in some foreign language, or languages. She kept her eyes closed, giving herself a few moments to make sense of everything. She tried to rub her eyes but found her hands were restrained.

"She's awake," said one of the voices.

Katja remained still, her eyes closed. She remem-bered the dock, the two men, *Mathias! I won't be afraid. Fear is the mind killer*, something she'd heard in a movie. *I've been in bondage, been punished and disciplined. Someone will come for me, Patrick and Dieter, they will come for me, all I need to do is stay alive.*

She opened her eyes and saw the Stuber brothers looming over her. They were in an ordinary room, she had no idea where. There was a Sumo wrestling match on the television. She was spread-eagled on a bed, restrained by leather wrist and ankle cuffs.

"Hope you don't find the hardware too uncomfort-able, but you're a rather dangerous cunt," Anton said.

Katja looked to the other man, the one she'd hit, and smiled when she saw the growing bruise from her back fist on the side of his face.

Max saw the smile, and lunged at her, "Bitch!"

Anton stopped him. "Not yet, we need to know some things." He reached down and stroked Katja's thigh, his thin lips forming a cruel smile as she flinched at his touch.

They'd removed her clothes before they restrained her to the bed. Katja focused, *A slave is not embarrassed by her nakedness.*

Anton ran his hand over her sex, feeling the soft red tufts amid the clean shaven skin. "Hey Max! The bitch shaves her cunt. Is that it? You shave it, or does that Dominatrix bitch you live with shave it?"

Katja held the man's gaze, but didn't answer.

"*Where* is Kurt?" Anton asked. "We know he entered the house."

She saw no need to lie, "Dead."

No one spoke. The only sound was the jabbering Japanese Sumo match on the television.

"Who killed him? How?"

Katja thought for a moment, there was no simple, single answer. The man was whipped and beaten to near death by her and Mistress Hannelore, and then dumped in the river. "We all killed him. He cried like a baby when I raped his ass."

"Fuckin' bitch!" Max leaned forward and slapped her repeatedly.

Twenty

After receiving Hannelore's phone call, they drove north all night, taking turns behind the wheel, keeping the BMW roaring down the *Autobahns*, only stopping at *Rastattes* for gas and coffee. Covering the 360 kilometers from south of *München* they stopped outside Frankfurt to meet an arms dealer, an old acquaintance of Patrick's.

"You know this man, this Gunther?" Dieter asked.

Patrick ate the last of his *Brötchen*. "We've done business, it's been a while, but I know he's still in the trade. Hannelore said the men that took Katja were pros. It was pure luck that Mathias ended up in the river, actually saved his ass. He said they came out of nowhere, stunned them, and took Katja away."

"Yes, I talked to Mathias. He is very sad, blames himself."

"I know how he feels, but there was nothing he could've done. Mathias is a good kid; he's smart and clever, you said he's a good deck hand, but against pros…" Patrick let the sentence hang.

"*Ja*, so we see this friend of yours, get what we need to equalize the odds."

"Yea, after seeing what they did to Kessler in Berlin, and now the move against Hannelore and Katja we need to go on the offensive." Patrick looked at Dieter. "I saw what your sister did in Rothenburg."

"Our father, a policeman, taught us to shoot, the skill, but the will, the determination to do it…is something in Falkes. I am with you, Steffi is with us; we will finish this. She will meet us in Hamburg."

"I don't doubt that, but this has turned into something more than finding an old Nazi document that may or may not exist. People are dying and we don't want any of them to be us."

"Then we need to end it."

Patrick nodded, "Agreed, let's go see Gunther."

A tall, strawberry blond girl met them at the door. She was bleary-eyed and her black transparent nightgown did little to disguise her voluptuous curves. "*Ja?*" Her German contained a heavy Russian accent.

"We have an appointment with *Herr* Hofman," Patrick said.

The girl brushed a wisp of hair from her eyes and backed up, allowing entrance. Her eyes roamed over Dieter as she seductively sucked at her lower lip.

"Natasha! Go! Make coffee." Gunter Hofman entered the room and the girl slinked away, casting a backwards glance at Dieter.

Gunther wore his usual ill-fitting suit, the coat too long on his short, corpulent form, his pudgy hands barely visible beneath the sleeves. He greeted Patrick warmly, like an old friend, but warily eyed Dieter. "Do I know you? You look familiar."

Dieter remained silent, staring down at the shorter man.

"Perhaps, perhaps not," Gunther shrugged, turning nervously to Patrick. "We thought you'd retired, were selling 'objects d'art' to well-heeled Japanese and American tourists. Yet here you are, buying weapons. Come in from the cold have you, back in the game?"

Patrick picked up a Glock 19, hefting the weapon in his hand, feeling its weight. "Something like that, I've taken a small job that's gotten out of hand." He placed it on the table and picked up a Glock 18.

Gunther enthusiastically pointed at the automatic in Patrick's hand. "The Glock 18, 9 mm, can take a 30-round clip, but not really concealable with the 30-round clip. The Daily Mirror in England called it 'the most terrifying gun in the world,' capable of a rate of fire of 1,100 rounds per minute. It's lightweight and reliable. The SAS use it, Israeli security forces, even our own GSG-9 carry it for combat ops."

Dieter took one of the guns in his large hand, giving Patrick an affirmative nod of the head.

Patrick turned to Gunther, "We'll take three, with the standard, and the 30-round clips, ammunition and paddle back holsters for each; how much?"

There followed a few moments of haggling about the money. While Gunther normally enjoyed the haggling he was unnerved by the presence of Dieter, and quickly settled on a price. Patrick counted out the Euros, and Gunther greedily stuck them in his pocket, leaving to get the guns. He returned with three boxes of factory fresh

Glocks, placing them on the table where Dieter began inspecting the merchandise, breaking down the weapons, and reassembling them with practiced skill.

"Walter King, or Walther König, you know him?" Patrick asked.

Gunther let out a contemptuous breath. "Not in your league Patrick, the man is a thug. Dangerous? Yes, certainly, because he has no honor, no pride in his work." Gunther looked at Patrick, "He won't be alone; he'll have people with him, someone to do his dirty work."

"We've met some already, and eliminated two," Patrick countered as he watched Dieter assemble the last weapon.

Gunther was silent, shooting inquisitive glances to Patrick and Dieter. When they offered no further information he merely shrugged. "He'll hire more, if he has to. They won't have your skills, your tradecraft, but they'll kill you just the same, if you give them the chance. I'd give you more information if I could, but these people live in the shadows…"

"I know my friend. What you've given us is appreciated." Patrick shook Gunther's hand while Dieter grabbed the boxes of Glocks.

As they went out the door Patrick heard Gunther offer a hearty "*Viel Gluck!*"

Patrick smiled, *Good Luck? The Glocks will improve our luck considerably.*

On the drive north Patrick tried to put it all together. He'd called König, using the contact info that König provided on their first meeting in *München*, but got a message service. It appeared to him that even though König had hired him he was now trying to cut him out of the deal. The attack on Hannelore was obviously an attempt to give König leverage in case Patrick got the document first. *As if there even IS a fucking document. This has turned into a bloody, deadly cluster fuck.* Patrick wished he could simply get Katja back, and put it all behind him, but he knew that wasn't possible. Things had to be finished now. He had to get the document, or settle accounts with König and his men. If there *was* a document he may have to do both. After he and Dieter got Katja back they would follow the trail back to Berchtesgaden, their destination before Katja's kidnapping. They'd check out the information on the maps they'd taken from Kessler in Berlin. Still, Patrick doubted that a sixty-plus year-old scrap of paper, even if it did exist, was going to be the answer. This episode was likely to end in more blood and death, and Patrick was determined that none of them would be victims.

He received a call from Hannelore assuring him that she and Mathias were safe, no one had made any moves on them, nor had anyone tried to contact them since Katja's abduction. Steffi had flown up from Nürnberg and Patrick felt better knowing that Dieter's cool, sharp-shooting sister was there. By this evening Steffi hoped to have information for Patrick, but was reluctant to say what she was doing or how she was getting the information. Patrick didn't press the issue, content to get any on-the-ground intelligence he could. Everyone had only one objective, get Katja safely back. If she could stay alive, he and Dieter would find her.

Twenty One

Katja lay quietly, bound to the bed. Her face was swollen and discolored from Max's assault. They hadn't asked her any more questions. She'd told them all she knew, seeing no reason to hide anything. She worried about Mathias and Mistress Hannelore. *Are they safe?*

Anton was flipping through the television channels, and thumbing through the local papers. "Nothing! Nothing! Two people are attacked, the girl is abducted, and the boy, who knows if he is drowned, missing, or what? And there's nothing, nothing on the television, nothing in the papers, on the news…nothing!" He threw the paper on the floor.

Max took a drink from a lukewarm bottle of beer. "Maybe that Domme bitch didn't report it. Maybe she's working some angle."

Anton stared at his brother in feigned surprise, "Do you think? Of course she's keeping a lid on it, probably trying to get help, figure out what to do."

"So what, we just sit here with the girl?"

"That's what König wants, a distraction so he can do whatever it is he's doing. I told him about his man Kurt, what they did to him. He didn't seem to care, probably figures it's one less person on the payroll."

Max drank more beer while Anton checked the news channels again.

Anton threw the car keys to Max. "I'm going back and take a look at the house, see if there's any activity."

"You don't want the car?"

"No, if that kid didn't drown in the river he may have seen our car, and made it back to the house. I'll take the *U-Bahn*, and walk around over there. Don't go anywhere, and don't call anybody, OK? On my way back I'll bring something to eat."

Max opened another beer. "Sure, sure, OK, get me one of those *Donner Kebabs*?"

All Max got was a nod of the head, and a wave of the hand from Anton, as he walked out the door. Max threw the bottle cap in the corner, took a drink, and walked to Katja.

He loomed over her as he finished his beer, tipping the bottle, letting the last dregs fall on her face. Max laughed as she blinked and twisted her head to the side. "We're all alone, just you and me for a while."

Through her swollen eyes Katja silently glared at him. Her silence and stoic behavior only angered him.

With his short, pudgy fingers Max reached down and grabbed one of her nipples. Holding the tender bud he slowly squeezed, smiling when his assault finally made her cry and try to pull away. "Not so tough are you?" With the nipple in his vise-like grip he pulled and twisted it away from her breast. Her efforts to control the pain only encouraged him, and he continued his abuse until her shrieks filled the room. Releasing the nipple he slapped her breast, his meaty hand leaving a large red mark. "Bet you're used to this shit, huh, bein' tied up and beat on, but Max don't play games. I'm gonna enjoy this, and I don't give a shit whether you do or not." His hands mauled her breasts, the fingers digging into the firm flesh as if he was kneading dough.

Katja couldn't fight the pain, and she twisted in vain to escape her tormenter. Max laughed and pulled his hands away, slapping her hard across her face. Katja began to sob, hopelessness overtaking her.

Suddenly she felt Max step back. She blinked away the tears, and looked up. Max stood over her, holding the beer bottle, leering at her. He continued to stare as he used the bottle to trace a line from her breasts, down her stomach, ending at her sex. He playfully probed at the outer edge with the bottle.

Katja glared at him, her dismay now replaced with anger. Her eyes burned into his and and she spoke slowly and confidently, "For this, you will die."

Max stopped, frozen in a split-second of hesitation as a glimmer of fear passed momentarily over his face. He looked the girl in the eyes, but her expression was one of determination. She closed her eyes, and laid her head back. "Fuck you!" Max yelled.

As the beer bottle disappeared between her legs Katja breathed deeply, slightly arching her back. Max's screaming and cursing faded as Katja sought refuge elsewhere. *I am with Mistress; we are together, warm and safe…*

Twenty Two

Hamburg Detective Angelika Müller set down her coffee and picked up the ringing phone, "Müller here."

"Angelika, it's Steffi, I'm in Hamburg."

A smile spread over Angelika's face at the thought of Steffi, her tall beautiful roommate from their Academy days. At only five-six Angelika was quite the contrast to the six foot Steffi, especially when Steffi wore the high heeled boots she favored. Yet, as Angelika's mother, herself short in stature always said, "It's a poor lumberjack who can't climb a fallen tree."

"Steffi, so good to hear from you, where are you, where can we meet?"

"I'm outside your building. I need your help to access some information. It's official…sort of."

"Meet me in the lobby."

*****

Steffi closed her eyes for a moment, and turned them back to the computer in Angelika's cubicle. It had been a long night and morning. She'd flown to Hamburg and met with Hannelore and Mathias. Now she was with her Hamburg Police contact. As the screen flickered and the image loaded she finally got a match from the crude fingerprint card she'd received from Hannelore.

"Definitely Kurt Rothe," Angelika said, "a minor criminal with some arrests and prison time." She held up the photo of a man tied down in a dimly lit room, "Yes, definitely him." Angelika hit the print key, and heard the paper sliding into the machine. While that was printing she started the search for any names associated with Kurt Rothe's nefarious past. She followed up with a search on each one of the names she found, printing out all the information she could access.

Determining the identities of the men who attacked Katja and Mathias had been easy. Angelika immediately recognized Mathias's descriptions as being the Stuber brothers. *The Stubers in Hamburg, away from their normal Bremen and Bremerhaven haunts, this is bad news.* She knew the Stubers, most in law enforcement did. They were regarded as dangerous; Anton because he was smart, and killed in cold blood, and Max because he was a street thug who liked to hurt people. *The Stubers: a sociopath and a sadist. Steffi, what are you doing?* Angelika looked at all the information they'd gathered, "What's going on, can I help?"

"Yes, where can I find the Stubers?"

Angelika considered the question. "Max likes to get juiced up, crank, meth, makes him even more dangerous. If he's in town he's probably getting it from Jacko."

"Jacko?" Steffi narrowed her eyes.

"Real name is Rudi Schwarz, calls himself Jacko, fancies himself a gang leader." Angelika laughed, "He's just a pusher with a few hangers-on. He'd be a logical supplier for Max."

"And we can find him, where?"

Angelika stood and slid her *Sig-Sauer* into her holster, "You're gonna love this."

*****

Even at mid-day the music in the club was too loud for Steffi's taste. The room had a pall of smoke and smelled of sweat and beer. Angelika passed through the tables to the far corner, where Jacko held court.

"Detective Angel," Jacko held up a beer in greeting, "who's your giant friend?" Jacko presided over his posse of two drug-addict girlfriends and three males in ragged t-shirts and too many tattoos and piercings.

Angelika and Steffi separated, standing at opposite sides of the table, and Angelika cocked her head in a 'what-did-I-tell-you' gesture. "This is detective Falke, from Nürnberg, she'd like some information."

"All the way from there, huh?" Jacko swallowed the last of his beer and slammed the bottle on the table. "Don't mean nothin' to me, Sorry Detective, but homey don't play dat."

Steffi furrowed her eyebrows at Jacko's reply.

"Too much American television," Angelika explained.

With stunning quickness Steffi grabbed Jacko's hair and slammed his face into the table.

As the other males started to rise, Angelika's hand

went to her *Sig-Sauer,* and they slowly took their seats.

Steffi jerked Jacko's head around to look him in the eyes. "I don't watch American television."

"You fuckin' bitch, you broke my nose!"

"I'm only getting started." Steffi pulled Jacko to his feet, still holding him by his hair and twisting his arm into an arm lock with her other hand.

The other patrons in the club stirred, but the looks given them by Angelika and Steffi had them turning away and minding their own business.

Steffi pushed Jacko down the hall and into the men's toilet. A startled patron standing at the urinal ran away with his cock in his hands when Steffi ordered, "Out!" She released her grip on Jacko and pushed him into the corner. "I want to know where the Stubers are."

Jacko wiped at the blood streaming from his nose and over his chin. "The Stubers? I don't—"

A vicious punch to his mid-section brought Jacko to his knees.

"Tell me what I want to know, and I'm gone. Your friends aren't coming to help you." Steffi delivered a savage kick to his thigh, insuring maximum use of the stiletto heel of her boot.

"OK," Jacko held up his hand. "OK, all I know is I got some stuff for Max, yea, but I don't know where he is, I just dropped it off."

Steffi grabbed his hair again, pulling his head up and cocking her other fist, ready to punch, "Where, who?"

"Emil, Emil Neumann, he runs a club—in the *Reeperbahn*. He might have a safe house the Stubers use."

"The club, what's the name?"

"The *Schwarz Kat*, the Black Cat." Jacko's eyes

pleaded, "Hey, it's all I know." He held up his hands, "Really, all I know."

Steffi stepped back and threw one hundred Euros on the floor. "Get drunk, get high, get laid, but get lost, for at least twenty four hours. Don't call anyone, don't talk to anyone. I find out you've talked to anyone about this and I'll be back—and finish it."

Jacko was on his knees, gathering up the bills from the floor as Steffi stalked out.

"Get what you needed?" Angelika asked, as they left the club.

Steffi smiled, "I did, you do know how to show a girl a good time."

Twenty Three

It wasn't a happy reunion when Patrick and Dieter arrived at Hannelore's house. Mathias was relieved to see Dieter, falling into his arms, and apologizing over and over about losing Katja.

Patrick embraced Hannelore, "How you holding up?"

She shrugged; her usual air of confidence and authority lacking. "I'm worried about her, Patrick. These men, what will they do to her? Is she even alive?"

"Yes, I believe she is alive, she has no value to them dead. No one's contacted you?"

"No, that's why I'm worried."

"Have you seen anyone around the neighborhood, out of place, maybe watching you or the house?"

Hannelore shook her head, "No."

Steffi soon arrived and they adjourned to the living room and Mathias related the incident on the dock. Patrick and Dieter let Mathias speak freely. When he finished, they began to ask questions. Which of the two spoke the most? Who seemed in control? Did Mathias notice if they were right-handed or left-handed? What weapons did they have? How far apart did they stand? The questions went on until Dieter felt Mathias couldn't give him any more.

Steffi passed around photos of the Stuber brothers.

Mathias nodded nervously, "Yes, that's them, the ones who…who…" Dieter reached over and clasped his hand on Mathias's shoulder.

Steffi continued, "Here are photos of Walther König, and some of those he's known to associate with."

Patrick picked up the photos and thumbed through them. "Yea, that's König."

He passed a second photo to Dieter, who took the picture of Erich Güler and smiled. "The man in the Rothenburg alley, he looks better here."

Patrick nodded, remembering that he still owed Steffi a Burberry coat.

"Erich Güler," Steffi said. "He often works with König."

"The Stubers," Patrick turned to Steffi. "Do we know where they might be?"

"Angelika said there was a man, Emil Neumann, who owns the *Schwarz Kat* club in the *Reeperbahn.* He's been known to associate with the Stubers and is believed to be their contact when they come to Hamburg. He may provide them a safe house when they're in town."

"The *Schwarz Kat*," Patrick said.

Hannelore snorted, "A cheap, no-class place to excite tourists."

*****

Anton returned to the room, dropping the grease-stained bag on a table. Max shoved in a hand, removing a *Donner Kebab*. "Mmmm, thanks," he mumbled through a mouthful of food.

Anton bent down and pulled Katja's face toward him. Her eyes glared into his. He reached down and took the beer bottle from between her legs.

Max swallowed a big piece of his sandwich, "She's alive; I didn't kill her."

"Good thing, Max, she doesn't do us any good dead. When König is through needing her we'll get rid of her. Get her off the bed, and let her go to the bathroom, but make sure you keep her hands cuffed. I saw what she did to you on the docks."

"Bitch got lucky," Max grumbled as he dropped his half-eaten sandwich on the table, and walked towards the bed.

Anton opened his cell phone and called König. "Yes, we still have her—Yea, I went by the house, nothing out of the ordinary, no police cars—Couple of guys walked in, but guys go there all the time, right?—Yea, we can hold her, for how long?—No, nobody knows where we are or who we are—Walther, trust me, we got our end covered here, OK?—Yea, we'll wait for your next call."

Max returned to the room and threw Katja on the bed, "That Walther on the phone?"

Anton nodded, "He wants us to hold the girl. Give her something to eat and drink, and chain her up again."

Katja eagerly consumed the half a sandwich Max threw at her. She needed to keep up her strength, needed to stay alive. *Patrick and Dieter will come for me; Mistress will make it happen.*

*****

Berchtesgaden, Bavaria

Walther König closed up his cell phone and turned back to his meal. "The Stubers have the girl that lives with the Dominatrix. That should keep Deveraux occupied."

Peter and Heinrich looked at each other, then to König. "So…does that get us closer to the document?" Peter asked.

"*Nein*, but it lets us continue the search without worrying about Deveraux."

Heinrich looked confused. "What are we looking for down here: the document, a map, what?"

"I'm not sure, but this is where Schleiman died, and where Kessler was heading, so whatever there is it must be down here, somewhere." König looked out the restaurant window, "We need to get into the tunnels, in that bunker where Schleiman died."

Both Peter and Heinrich looked doubtful. "That's not so easy. They've been off limits for years, blocked, sealed up."

König silenced them with a look. "Schleiman got in, so will we." He picked up his cell phone and called Hamburg.

*****

Patrick, Dieter and Hannelore were going over the documents and photos provided by Angelika and Steffi when the phone rang. Hannelore answered, her eyes widening at the flat, dead-sounding voice on the other end of the line.

"We have the girl."

Hannelore put her hand over the phone. "Patrick! It's them."

Patrick took the phone, "Talk."

"Deveraux? Do you have the document?"

"No. Let the girl go, she's not involved."

"That's not what I hear, Deveraux, I heard she killed Kurt. I'll keep her, just to make sure you hold up your end of the deal. Bring me the document, and you get the girl."

"There *is* no fucking document."

"You'd better hope there's a document, for the girl's sake. We'll be in touch, don't do anything stupid." The line went dead.

Patrick looked at Hannelore, "She's alive."

Hannelore was torn between sorrow and anger. "What are we going to do?"

"Do what you have to do," Steffi said. "Angelika and I will clean up the loose ends, cover your tracks."

"Then we are going to the *Reeperbahn*, to the *Schwarz Kat* club." Everyone turned to see Dieter sliding one of the Glocks into the holster behind his back.

Twenty Four

"Give me 15 minutes to change," Hannelore said.

Patrick shook his head, "You're not going anywhere."

Hannelore's look was pure defiance. "And where would I be safer than with you and Dieter?"

It's exactly the kind of thing Heike would have said, Patrick thought. He looked to Dieter who merely shrugged. "OK, 15 minutes."

Dieter yelled for Mathias who quickly came into the room. He tossed him the car keys, "Bring the car around." He turned to Patrick, "Hannelore, she may be useful, a diversion?"

"We've lost Katja, I don't want anyone else hurt."

Dieter dropped two fully loaded clips into his pocket. "We won't be getting hurt."

Hannelore looked at the reflection in the mirror. For to-night she'd chosen a knee-length, black leather pencil skirt, dark hosiery and knee-high leather boots with a four-inch stiletto heel. The crisp, white, low-cut blouse contrasted nicely with the dark skirt, stockings and boots, giving her the severe look she wanted. She debated, finally deciding on the darker eye shadow and mascara. After all, they were going to the *Reeperbahn*, and she was a famous Domme, with a reputation to maintain. How she could assist Patrick and Dieter she didn't exactly know, but if there was a way, anything she could do to get Katja back…Yes, she was worried about Katja, but she had confidence in Patrick and Dieter. After a final appraisal in the mirror she grabbed her purse, and selected a leather jacket with a fur collar.

The others nodded approvingly when she made her appearance. Hannelore handed a leather collar to Mathias, "Put it on."

Mathias nervously looked to Dieter.

"Do it," Dieter said.

"It will look more natural if I have a submissive with me, it would be expected." Hannelore moved behind Mathias, helping him fasten the collar.

Patrick looked at Dieter, "Do we have a plan?"

"We go to the club, see *Herr* Neumann, find the Stubers and get Katja."

"It's simple and direct, I like it." Patrick turned to the others, "Any questions? No—then let's go."

Mathias started for the door, but was restrained by Hannelore. "Behind me tonight *Liebchen*, remember your place."

Dieter's laugh made Mathias blush.

*****

Dieter parked the car on a side street a block from the *Schwarz Kat* club.

"We'll go in separately. Dieter and I will go in first. Hannelore, you and Mathias go in a few minutes later. It's best if they don't know you're with us. Keep your eyes and ears open, and watch your back. Act naturally, but be ready for anything." Patrick looked up and down the street. "If we get separated we'll meet over there," he pointed to a small bar down the street, "that will be our rendezvous point. We want to do this with as little trouble as possible. If shooting breaks out, drop to the floor, when it's over, when it's safe, get to the rendezvous point and wait. If you can't do this, then stay here and wait."

Hannelore was resolved, "I'm going in."

Mathias shook his head in agreement.

Patrick got out of the car. "Wait for ten minutes, and then go in. It's a Saturday night, you're out cruising the *Reeperbahn* with your sub in tow, you're checking out the action at the club. Don't pay any attention to us. If it looks like we're in trouble, start a diversion, slap Mathias around, do something to give Dieter and I the edge to act."

Hannelore put out a hand to grasp Patrick's arm. "Mathias and I will be fine. Do what you have to do to get Katja back."

Twenty Five

The *Schwarz Kat* club was only a small step up from a seedy sex club. A flashing neon sign advertised 'Live Sex On Stage,' with a billboard showing a well-endowed, dark-skinned beauty holding a large snake. The doorman spewed the usual patter to lure in tourists: "Live sex on stage, see Sharka dance with the serpent, see Udo's twenty centimeter cock!"

Dieter's eyebrows arched in mock surprise, "Twenty centimeters, very impressive."

Patrick agreed, "Eight inches, that would be something."

The doorman ushered them inside, promising them a great show. As Dieter paid their cover charge Patrick quickly surveyed the club. A small stage occupied one end of the room. The bar was in the back, off to the side. There was a door that probably led to rooms or offices in the back. The rest of the interior was taken up with small tables jammed together, some on the floor, and the rest in two levels of risers. It was a small room, yet

Greg Causey

everyone was assured a good view. Dieter tipped the man and he led them to one of the upper tables by the wall.

"Good choice," Patrick said, as they both ordered beers. "No one at our back, we have a good view of the room, and a clear field of fire." Their beers arrived, and they nursed the drinks while they watched the club fill up. The live show was scheduled to start in 20 minutes.

Down the street from the club Hannelore stopped to retrieve her cigarette holder and cigarettes from her purse. She handed Mathias the lighter, and he lit her cigarette. "Follow my lead; remember that tonight you are my submissive, act the part."

Mathias submissively bowed his head, "Yes, Mistress."

She affectionately patted his cheek. "We do this for Katja, and to help Patrick and Dieter."

As they approached the club the doorman began his spiel, "Live sex on stage, see Sharka dance with the serpent, see Udo's twenty—Mistress Hannelore! Maybe you don't remember—"

"Of course, Peter, how good to see you."

Peter beamed with the realization that Mistress Hannelore remembered him. "You are coming to the club?"

"Yes," she pointed to Mathias standing silently behind her. "I promised my submissive a night out."

"We are honored to have you here." Peter personally escorted her inside, showing her to a table.

"Perhaps something in the middle?" she suggested.

"Of course, Mistress."

Peter seated them, snapping his fingers for a waiter to take their order.

"Enjoy the show, Mistress."

"Thank you, Peter."

Patrick and Dieter watched them arrive and take their seats. "Right in the middle, if they have to create a diversion everyone will notice," Dieter said.

Hannelore quickly made herself the center of attention. Soon all eyes were watching the stunning brunette with the young submissive. He lit her cigarettes, picked her napkin up from the floor, moved her ashtray, and sat submissively as she caressed him like a much beloved pet. The tourists in the crowd enjoyed this show-before-the-show, whispering among themselves, pointing to the woman and young man in the center of the club.

"Do you think she's going to be in the show?"

"Stanley, see if you can take a picture!"

"The folks back home in Ohio aren't gonna believe this!"

Dieter and Patrick watched it with amusement.

"She's good."

"She's Mistress Hannelore."

As the lights in the murky club dimmed even further a voice announced, "The exotic dancing of— Ramona!" The curtains on the small stage parted to reveal a willowy, partially clad, and only moderately endowed, bleach blonde, gyrating to music blaring over the house sound system.

With all eyes affixed to the erotic scene on the stage Dieter rose and walked to the empty bar where a disinterested bar tender lumbered up to take his drink order. Dieter reached over, grabbing the man's shirt, pulling him over the bar. Face to face, he looked the man in the eyes. "I need to see *Herr* Neumann, now." He pushed the terrified bar tender back across the bar.

From his left Dieter saw movement as one of the house bouncers approached, "*Herr* Neumann isn't here tonight; I think you'd better—"

Dieter's quick punch to the man's solar plexus doubled him over. Before the man could rise Dieter grabbed the man's neck, shoving his face into the bar, and breaking his nose.

The bartender reached for something under the bar, but felt a gun rudely jammed into his ribs. He saw Patrick standing beside him, shaking his head 'No.' The music blared, the girl on stage was now totally nude, and no one was paying attention to the bar.

Dieter pulled up the man with the bleeding nose. "*Herr* Neumann, now!"

The stunned bouncer looked at both Patrick and Dieter, fearfully nodded, and led them through the door at the end of the bar.

A few steps down a dingy hallway lined with beer cases took them to another door. The bouncer with the bloody face knocked on the door. From inside came a, "*Ja, Ja,* come in."

Dieter kicked the door open, throwing the bouncer ahead of him into the room. Patrick followed quickly with his gun aimed at a startled Emil Neumann.

"What are you? Do you know—" Neumann's outburst was silenced as Dieter's huge fist collided with his face. Blood spurted over the papers on Neumann's desk. Dieter grabbed Neumann by the lapels of his suit and pulled him upright.

"The Stubers, where are they?"

Neumann's face revealed fear and confusion. *Who are these men? What do they want?*

Dieter repeated the question. "The Stubers, where are they?"

Neumann shook his head. "I, I, don't…know."

Dieter looked to Patrick who grabbed a leather jacket and wrapped it over the end of his Glock. He placed the barrel at the bouncer's knee.

"The Stubers?" Dieter growled.

Neumann shook his head, his eyes wide with fear.

Without a second's pause Patrick fired a round into the bouncer's knee. The man screamed and fell to the floor. Neumann went weak in the knees, wetting himself.

Dieter's nose crinkled with disgust as he released his grip, letting the man fall to the floor.

Patrick walked to Neumann and held the gun to his knee. "Give us the Stubers, now! Or shop for a cane in the morning. I promise you, the Stubers are the least of your worries. They'll be dead tomorrow, *you* could still be alive."

His hands were shaking so badly Emil Neumann was barely able to write down the Stuber's address as he gave up all he knew.

Dieter pocketed the paper. "Don't call them, don't follow us, don't call anyone. We are finished here, but if we have to come back…"

Neumann excitedly nodded, "Yes, yes, I understand."

Dieter picked up a nearby towel, and threw it to the bouncer who used it to stem the bleeding from his shattered knee. He turned to the quaking Neumann,

"You're going to need a new man; next time hire someone better."

Patrick holstered his weapon, and he and Dieter walked out of the office. They made their way through the crowd and out the door. No one gave them any notice, the crowd's eyes fixed to the spectacle unfolding on the stage of a voluptuous redhead going down on Udo's massive cock, now swollen much beyond its twenty centimeters.

Hannelore and Mathias watched them leave, but remained in their seats. The show was drawing to a close, and they would leave with the crowd. Hannelore looked behind her, but saw nothing out of the ordinary. *Did they get any information?*

Twenty Six

Patrick and Dieter waited at the rendezvous point, ordering only coffee. Both men needed to keep their edge for what they were going to do in the next few hours. Patrick looked at his watch, again. "Where are they?"

At that moment Hannelore walked through the door, Mathias obediently trailing behind. They joined the men at their table. "Did you find out anything? Do you know where she is?"

"We may know where she is," Patrick said.

"What about the club?" Dieter asked. "Was there anything going on after we left?"

"No, we didn't see anything. It seemed to be a typical evening." Hannelore eyed Dieter, "*Was* there trouble?"

Dieter chuckled, "Not for us, but we left some damage behind."

Hannelore took a cigarette from her purse, and Mathias offered a light. "So, are you going to get her?"

Patrick nodded. "Yes, but you and Mathias need

to stay behind this time. Dieter and I can't do this, and worry about you two."

A pout framed Hannelore's face, but she knew Patrick was right. "When do you do this thing?"

"Now, tonight," Patrick finished his coffee. "I don't want you to go home, not yet, not until we can go with you. Check into a hotel, stay out of sight, until Dieter or I contact you."

Hannelore crushed out her cigarette. "Just get her back, safe, please."

Dieter dropped Hannelore and Mathias where they could catch a cab to a hotel, waiting until they were safely in the cab, and on their way. Before leaving Hannelore leaned out the window, "Please be careful, but bring her back."

Confident that Hannelore and Mathias would be safe, Dieter turned the car around, and drove to the address provided by Emil Neumann. A block behind Steffi slowly pulled out, and followed at a safe distance.

"You think Neumann told the truth?" Dieter said.

"It'll go bad for him if he didn't," Patrick replied.

"Think he called them, tipped them off?"

Patrick chuckled, "I doubt it. You literally scared the piss out of him. I've never seen anyone give it up so quickly."

"What about the Stubers, how are we going to handle them?"

"Go in hard and fast, quick and lethal, take them out before they can react, or harm Katja."

Dieter's voice was hard, "Good plan, I like it."

It took only thirty minutes to get to the address

provided by Neumann. Late-night traffic was light, and the industrial area they found themselves in was as good as deserted.

Dieter drove by the address, and parked a block away, around the corner, deciding to approach on foot. They watched the building for fifteen minutes; all seemed quiet. A second story window illuminated with the flickering of someone watching late night television.

"Neumann said that would be them, second floor, facing the street. According to him there's no one else in there."

Dieter murmured his agreement, and pointed to a door on the side of the building.

"OK, let's go." Staying in the shadows they made their way across the street, and down the block, stopping at the door. Again, they paused and waited, but heard nothing.

Patrick tried the door handle, turning slowly, "Locked." He produced lock picks, and in seconds freed the lock.

"You have skills," Dieter whispered.

"Old habits, they stay with you."

They slowly eased the door open; thankful it was a quiet mechanism. Once inside they paused to listen, and to let their eyes adjust to the interior darkness of the building. Both men had their weapons out and ready. Dieter pointed to the stairwell. Patrick quietly moved to the stairs while Dieter kept his weapon trained on the stairwell. Once Patrick was in place he provided cover for Dieter to join him. They heard the faint sound of the television.

Patrick pointed to the stairs. They were cement,

both men smiled. At least there wouldn't be the creaking of wood or metal to give them away. Slowly they worked their way up the stairs. *The brave knights ascending the tower to rescue the fair maiden,* Patrick thought.

*****

Max Stuber ate the last piece of pizza, wiping his hands on his pants. Anton stretched out, half-asleep, on the sofa. Their prize, Katja, was restrained to the bed. This was the part of the work that Max hated the most, the waiting. He liked action, especially when it involved violence. To-night he passed the time watching erotic music videos. This job paid well, at least for what they were doing. Taking the boy and the girl had been easy. They didn't know what happened to the boy, but they had the girl, and this provided König all the leverage he needed for what-ever it was he was doing. Apart from the few minutes of action on the dock it was a boring job.

Max looked forward to finishing off the girl. That bit of closure would make it all worthwhile for him. Anton wouldn't mind, he'd let him do the wet work at the end. Anton knew what Max needed, action, something to hap-pen.

*****

Patrick and Dieter slowly moved down the hall until they were at the door. They heard music coming from the television, late night music videos of naked girls no doubt.

Patrick dropped silently to the floor, and peered beneath the door. Through the crack he saw a man's feet hanging down from a chair. He didn't see any indication of the other Stuber or Katja. He motioned to Dieter that there was one man seated in a chair. Patrick pointed up and down, and remained on the floor. Dieter acknowledged, they would go in high and low.

Dieter backed up to the wall. Patrick raised three fingers...three. Dieter lifted his leg, his fisherman's boot poised to kick in the door. Patrick dropped a finger…two. Patrick dropped the last finger…one.

Restrained, Katja was a captive witness to the horrific retribution. Although it was over in mere seconds it seemed to unfold in slow motion before her eyes. Dieter's huge foot shattered the handle, crashing open the flimsy door. Patrick exploded into the room from a crouch, keeping low. He knew where one Stuber was, and quickly found his target. A startled Max dropped his beer, and Patrick placed three shots across his torso, the rounds throwing Max backwards and onto the floor.

Dieter's huge bulk filled the door, his outstretched arms ending in the deadly Glock.

Anton rose from the couch, reaching for his weapon as Dieter double-tapped him with a kill shot to the head and one to the chest. Anton's lifeless form crumpled to the floor, his weapon still on the table, a lifetime away.

Patrick rose to his feet, quickly scanning the scene. "Check the other rooms."

While Dieter cleared the small apartment Patrick went to Katja.

"I knew you would come," she cried. "I knew you would come for me."

When Patrick removed the last restraints she collapsed, shaking and sobbing, into his arms.

Dieter brought Katja her clothes, and wrapped his strong arms around her. "It's over now, we will take you home." Dieter broke the embrace and went to the window.

"Anything?" Patrick asked.

"Nothing, but we made a lot of noise. Even in this deserted area someone may have heard something." He took out his cell phone and called Steffi. "We have her, it's over."

"Wipe down anything you may have touched on your way out," Steffi replied. "I'll give you a few minutes, and then I'll call this in to my contact. Don't worry; I'll keep you out of it, just say that I got a tip from an informant that a hit went down, not exactly untrue."

Patrick turned to Katja. "Get dressed, we have to leave, quickly."

Katja pulled on her pants, "Mistress Hannelore, she is safe?"

Patrick dried her tears. "Everyone is safe, in a little while we will all be together. We need to clean up any signs that we were here, and we need to leave."

Dieter picked up the shell casings from their Glocks while Patrick stripped the sheets from the bed where Katja was restrained.

"Katja, did you touch anything, here, in the room?"

"Maybe in the bathroom, I…"

"I'll wipe it down," Patrick grabbed a towel.

"Anything else?"

Katja wordlessly pointed to the beer bottle on the bed.

Dieter picked up the bottle, and threw it in a pillowcase. His face showed the disgust at what had transpired with the bottle.

Patrick emerged from the bathroom, throwing the towel, bed sheets, and restraints into the pillowcase.

Across the room Katja stood over the lifeless form of Max Stuber.

Patrick held her, "It's all right Katja. He can't hurt you now, he's dead."

Katja's unfeeling eyes met Patrick's, "I know, I told him he would be."

Twenty Seven

Dieter pulled the car into a 24-hour gas station, and waited while Patrick went inside. He used the time to call Hannelore, "Yes, we have her, she's OK, yes, Patrick and I are fine."

Hannelore breathed a sigh of relief. "Please put her on, let me speak to her."

Dieter handed the phone to Katja.

"Mistress, I knew they would come, I knew you would find me."

"Did they hurt you?"

"I just want to come home."

"Yes, *Liebchen*, we will be together soon."

Katja gave the phone back to Dieter as Patrick returned to the car. Patrick handed Katja a bottle of water. As she drank the water he twisted the cap off a small bottle of *Chantre' Weinbrand*, and offered it to her. Without being told she took a drink, feeling the flush of the Brandy through her body. She handed the bottle back to Patrick who tipped the bottle in a mock toast, taking a drink himself. Katja smiled, and relaxed into the seat.

Dieter was still on the phone with Hannelore. "Yes, Angelika showed up to cover our tracks, her help is appreciated. Where are you? Good, we'll meet you there, spend the night, and everyone can go home tomorrow. Yes, we'll be there soon. Can you have some food and drinks? *Ja, Bis Später*."

Patrick handed the bottle back to Katja. "So where did Hannelore go?"

Dieter's lips split into a large smile, "*Die Vier Jahreszeiten*."

Patrick's head fell back on the headrest, "The Four Seasons, only the best for Hannelore."

*****

When the door opened Katja literally fell into Mathias's arms, the two holding each other, weeping tears of joy. Both professed their worry over the unknown fate of the other.

Hannelore embraced Patrick and Dieter, thanking them for their friendship, courage and strength. She didn't ask for details of the rescue, simply content that everyone was safe.

Katja pulled herself from Mathias's embrace, and went to Hannelore. They passionately clutched one another, Hannelore covering the girl's face with kisses, and brushing back her red hair. "*Liebchen*, I was so worried about you."

"I knew you would find me, Mistress, that they would come for me," she looked to Dieter and Patrick.

Hannelore led her away, "Let me put you in the bath, and get you some clean clothes."

Dieter pulled Mathias close to him, warmly embracing the boy.

Patrick settled into a chair. The table before him held Single Malt Scotch, French Cognac, *Schnapps*, a selection of chilled beers, and a platter of sandwiches; Hannelore was an excellent hostess, even on the run. He poured a large measure of the Scotch into a cut crystal glass, letting the strong liquid roll down the back of his throat. *A few days ago it was so simple, a modest, and safe living selling antiques. Now, now I'm up to my ass in it again.*

He was left alone as Hannelore and Katja, and Dieter and Mathias, filled plates with food and drink and went to their separate rooms. Patrick kicked off his shoes and sprawled out on the couch.

A soft knock on the door bought him upright with the Glock in his hand.

"It's me, Steffi," came the voice beyond the door.

He stood to the side of the door and opened it. When Steffi entered the room and closed the door behind her he relaxed, and holstered his weapon. "Sorry, habits, why I'm still alive."

She shed her coat and poured herself a *Schnapps*. "I understand." She downed the drink and poured another, holding it up, "Good work tonight, quick, clean." She swallowed her second drink and grabbed a sandwich.

Patrick poured his second scotch and returned the toast. "Thank you, and for Rothenberg."

"Angelika is managing the crime scene," Steffi rummaged through the beers, deciding on a *Becks*, "she'll keep us out of it." She relaxed in her chair and eyed Patrick. "This situation you have, it is complicated, yes?"

Patrick laughed, "Americans would call it a cluster fuck."

"You have no idea who is behind it? Other than faceless Arabs?"

"You know what I know," Patrick took his own sandwich.

Steffi leaned forward and pulled off her boots. "Have you had dealings with Arabs?"

Patrick was pensive for a moment, "*Who*, exactly, is asking, Detective Falke, or Dieter's sister?"

She removed her gun and badge, placing them on the table, "Dieter's sister—and your friend."

"There was a *thing*, an arms deal; we were double-crossed by the contact in Beirut, an Arab." Patrick looked directly into Steffi's blue eyes, "I was sent to sanction the contact, settle things. We couldn't let people think we could be cheated."

"And you did this? For the IRA?"

"It was a long time ago. A lifetime…"

Several moments of silence passed.

Steffi stood, and unbuttoned her blouse, casually throwing it over the back of her chair. Her pants quickly followed, until she stood, clad only in matching bra and panties. With two quick steps she was on the sofa, her hands clutching Patrick's face as her lips met his.

There hadn't been anyone since Heike, but even before Heike, Patrick had never met anyone like Steffi. She was strong, confident, beautiful, and she was clearly a woman who took whatever she wanted.

She backed away, her legs still straddling his lap.

Her breasts jutted forth when she reached around to unfasten her bra. After the bra was discarded she swept her blonde mane from her shoulders.

Patrick sat, speechless, as she leaned forward and ripped open his shirt, the buttons flying off in various directions.

Steffi slid down his body, her teeth capturing one of his nipples. Her eyes glowed with excitement when he grimaced at her love bites. She leaned back and shook her head, her blonde hair cascading over her shoulders as golden lava. Her hands grabbed at his belt, "Off," she commanded. Steffi backed away as Patrick shed his pants. For a moment they stood, naked, facing each other.

They moved as one, toward each other. Patrick grabbed her blond tresses and pulled her head back, smothering her with a kiss. For once, Steffi yielded, falling into Patrick, letting him take the lead.

The lovers fell onto the sofa, Patrick on top, Steffi clutching furiously at his back. Patrick traced kisses over her shoulders and down the crevice of her breasts. He felt her hands on his shoulders, pushing him down, lower…

It was an intimacy he hadn't felt for ages, a woman's flesh, the softness of her skin, the scent of her. Her sensual crescent of blond curls tickled his nose, and he felt her stiffen and gasp as he planted gentle kisses on her sex.

Patrick threw aside his years of loneliness and the recent stench of death, now there was only a need, for this woman.

Steffi shuddered and pushed him away, turning on him and pinning him under her. Her hand roughly grabbed his cock, squeezing it, "We do this my way."

Patrick's hand grasped the back of her neck, pulling her forward into another kiss, roughly claiming her lips.

She met his kiss, but didn't release her grip, feeling his shaft grow in her hand. Her hair brushed his face as she wrenched free from the kiss. *I'll take my prize now.* Steffi rose up, arching her back, sliding down Patrick's torso and positioning herself over his stiffened cock. She took a deep breath and plunged down, lowering herself, burying her prize deep within her fiery slit.

Patrick's breathing was labored as she literally rode him, taking her pleasure, and giving him the same in return. There was no lost Will, no death, no killing. For the first time—in a long time, he felt alive.

Twenty Eight

When they woke Hannelore ordered room service. Patrick had to admit; Hannelore had style, appreciated the finer things, and knew how to live. The breakfast was delicious, but the conversation guarded. Katja offered few details of her experience, and Patrick and Dieter didn't speak of the violence meted out on the Stubers.

Dieter noted Patrick's shirt, minus many of the buttons now strewn about the floor, and laughed, slapping Patrick on the shoulder, "This you must do on your own, I cannot have your back."

Patrick held up a hand, "I didn't mean to—"

"You think you could have stopped her?" Dieter shook his head, "She will have what she wants." His eyes settled on Patrick's, "Maybe you need this, yes?" He slapped Patrick on the back and went to join Mathias.

"He's right," Hannelore softly touched Patrick's arm. "It's not good for you to be alone, it's not what I want—or what Heike would have wanted. You've honored her in life and death, perhaps it's time..."

"Maybe," Patrick said, "maybe you're right. Only not now, now I still have unfinished business."

Hannelore kissed him on the cheek, "I understand. When this is over though, you must take care of you. Life goes on."

After breakfast, Dieter and Mathias brought the car around while Hannelore settled the hotel bill. The ride to Hannelore's house was quiet, everyone relieved the ordeal was over.

Dieter dropped Patrick and Steffi off a block from Hannelore's house so they could approach on foot and secure the area. Meanwhile Dieter made two passes around the block looking for anything out of the ordinary. Satisfied that the area was secure Patrick phoned Dieter, telling him to come in.

"Was all that necessary?" Hannelore asked.

Patrick was firm, "For now, yes, until this is over we don't need to take any chances. I suggest you hold off seeing clients for a while, until we know it's absolutely safe."

Once they were settled in the house Dieter and Mathias left to clean up the mess made by the Stuber's on Dieter's boat.

Hannelore gave Katja a sedative, and put her to bed. "Do you think she needs a doctor?"

"I think so," Patrick said. "It looks to me like they roughed her up a bit. Do you know someone that could come and see her here, keep it quiet?"

"Of course, I'll see to that this afternoon, after she's had some rest."

"I don't want to leave you here alone when Dieter and I go back to Bavaria."

"*Liebchen*, I'll have Mathias and Katja."

"That's not good enough. Maybe Angelika can stay here?"

"I'll call her, if you think it's necessary."

"I do."

*****

Angelika arrived later that afternoon. The dark circles under her eyes spoke of a long night. Everyone assembled in Hannelore's living room, Dieter and Mathias having returned from the boat. "You caused a lot of trouble last night," she said, eyeing Patrick and Dieter. "Not that we mind the Stubers gone, but still, it's made a lot of work for us. How is Katja?"

Hannelore poured coffee. "Fine, a doctor looked at her, she has some cuts and bruises, but she will be fine, at least physically."

Angelika touched Hannelore's arm, "If you need someone for her, some counseling, I know someone…"

"Thank you."

"I know you asked if I could stay with you, while…" Angelika looked at Dieter and Patrick, anticipating the further havoc they might wreak in Bavaria, "but I don't believe it is a good idea, if I may offer a suggestion?"

"Please."

"I know someone, in private security. He is very good, quite capable, ex-GSG-9. I trust him." Angelika glanced at Dieter who remained expressionless. "His name is Manfred Kopp."

Hannelore looked to Dieter who slowly nodded his head, 'Yes'.

"Yes, Angelika, thank you that will be fine."

"I'll make the call." Angelika took her phone and left the room.

Patrick turned to Dieter. "Will they be OK?"

"It will be fine," Dieter said, "we can do our job; they will be safe."

Angelika returned to the room, "*Herr* Kopp will be here in the morning."

"Tomorrow," Patrick said, "we go back to Bavaria." *Hopefully to end this.*

*****

Manfred Kopp sat in his car, watching the house. At seven a.m. he saw two men leave the house, get in a BMW, and drive away. *Dieter, my old comrade, what battles are we fighting now?* For another ten minutes he waited and watched. Satisfied that nothing was amiss he took his bags from the trunk and walked to the door. Hannelore met him and escorted him to the living room, offering him coffee, which he graciously accepted.

Hannelore sat opposite, and visually appraised her new house guest. At five-nine he was shorter than both Patrick and Dieter, but under his well cut dark suit and black turtleneck she discerned a compact, well-muscled frame. His hair was close-cropped and graying, yet his gray-green eyes held a young and playful quality.

"Thank you for coming, Angelika spoke highly of you."

Manfred relaxed in his chair. "I have worked with

her and also hold her in high regard. She explained something of your situation and needs."

Hannelore paused, "Do you know Dieter, *Herr* Falke?"

Manfred's eyes said 'Yes', but he didn't answer the question. "If I might see the house and talk to the occupants?"

"Of course."

Twenty Nine

Satisfied that Hannelore and the rest would be safe with *Herr* Kopp, Patrick and Dieter drove all day, stopping for the night at a small village outside Berchtesgaden. Over breakfast the next morning they reviewed the maps they'd retrieved from *Herr* Kessler's Berlin apartment.

The maps consisted of a simple commercial map of *Berchtesgadener Land*, with city plans, a panorama of the Alps, and hiking trails. The Alps panorama side had the *Obersalzberg* and *Kehlstein* area circled with a black marker.

As a fisherman well acquainted with maps and navigation Dieter was not impressed, "Gives us nothing."

"Narrows it down to one mountain in Europe," Patrick quipped.

Dieter snorted his disapproval, and drank more coffee.

"Yea," Patrick agreed, "that much we could've guessed."

Dieter shrugged.

Patrick continued, "This other side, the hiking trails, gives us a bit more. It looks like Schleiman made notes here and here." Patrick brushed his *Brötchen* crumbs from the map, and pointed to a place on one of the marked hiking trails. "This point here, it's almost due south of the *Platterhof* hotel, which was one of the entrances into the *Obersalzberg* bunker system."

Dieter studied the map. "You think Schleiman found an unmarked section of the tunnel system, something no one knew about?"

"Maybe, or maybe Kessler told him where to look. According to the background info I got from König, Kessler was an engineer who helped the Allies map out, and seal up, many of these networks at the end of the war."

Dieter remained silent, and looked doubtful.

Patrick put jam on the last of his *Brötchen*, and stuffed it in his mouth. "OK, I'm not sure I believe it all either, lost wills, hidden tunnels, I don't think there's any hidden secrets left. But *somebody* believes *something*, because Schleiman, Kessler, two of König's men, and the Stubers are all dead. If this is a wild goose chase…well, it's a deadly one."

Dieter nodded in the affirmative, "*Ja*. So we …"

"We go to Berchtesgaden, poke around, find out if anyone knew about Schleiman or what he was doing, we take a little hike, and see if we can find anything on the hiking trail."

"Agreed, and we watch for König," Dieter added.

*****

They arrived at Berchtesgaden early that morning, and parked near the train station. Each man had a task.

Dieter would prowl around town, making inquiries about Schleiman. His death had been big, local news so maybe someone knew something, and would be willing to talk. It was a long shot, but they didn't have much else.

Patrick would play the tourist. He waited at the train station, tourist-like, for the bus to take him to the *Hintereck* and the *Obersalzberg*. He bought tourist guide books and a map in the train station gift shop. As a precaution he'd left the original maps from Kessler's apartment locked in the car, and now he looked on his tourist map, and mentally memorized the same locations and markings as on Schleiman's original map. The bus arrived twenty minutes later and, along with several other tourists, he boarded.

It was a beautiful, spring day in Bavaria, and the bus ride to the *Obersalzberg* was scenic. The river coursing through town was blue green, and the red tile roofs stood out against a blue sky. Patrick ruminated on how beautiful and idyllic it must have looked to the National Socialist Party leaders when they first came here to put their own infamous stamp on the sleepy Bavarian village.

When the bus arrived at its destination Patrick disembarked and mingled. In a souvenir shop he bought a bottle of water, a walking stick, and a cheap disposable camera. Consulting his map he set out on the hiking trail. He walked the trail, stopping every once in a while to take a drink or shoot the obligatory 'picturesque photograph.' Satisfied that no one was following, he walked on, occasionally checking his back.

Dieter roamed the town, stopping at cafés and bars

to chat people up, asking if they knew anything about the archeologist killed in the tunnel collapse. All had heard of the incident, most believing it to be another case of a zealot relic-hunter searching for Nazi treasure or artifacts. After the Allied bombings and the post-war plundering there wasn't much left of the Nazi presence on the *Obersalzberg.* The Bavarian government finished the job by blowing up what was left, except for Hitler's Eagle's Nest, the *Kehlstein Haus.* Most believed that Schleiman had been a foolish old man looking for things that weren't there, although those who'd seen him in the local restaurants said that he was pleasant and agreeable enough.

By mid-afternoon Dieter didn't know much more than when he'd started. The endless coffees and beers over conversations were straining his bladder. He found a quiet place, and took out his cell phone to call Patrick, hoping that he could make the connection. The technology Gods were kind, it seemed that neither were in a hole.

Patrick quickly came on, "Find anything?"

"Nothing, most people say he was a nice enough old man, just chasing foolish dreams that got him killed."

Patrick chuckled on the other end. "That could describe all of us in this venture."

"You?"

"This isn't the most detailed map, but I think I'm getting close to the points marked on Schleiman's map."

"You want help?"

Patrick thought for a moment. "Just drive up to the *Hintereck* and hang out. Watch my back." He knew he had only a couple of hours of good daylight left, but according to Schleiman's map he felt he was close. He tried to locate his position relative to the *Platterhof* Hotel, to the north of him. What he was looking for wouldn't be on the trail itself; that would be too obvious. He looked for signs that some-one had left the hiking path, and walked off, towards the north.

He saw it, almost exactly where Schleiman marked it on the map. The grass was slightly trampled down, brush and twigs broken, as if someone had come through roughly, *perhaps carrying equipment?* Patrick took a picture, and looked around to see if he was alone. Seeing no one else on the trail he followed the signs to the north. It wouldn't have taken an expert tracker to follow the boot marks and broken brush.

The trail led to a small clump of trees and bushes. Patrick made a circle around the area but didn't find any signs leading out. He stepped back to look. It seemed oddly out of place, this clump of trees and strategically planted bushes, not as old as some of the old-growth surrounding forest, but newer than some of the landscaping along the hiking trail itself. He wasn't a horticulturist, but estimated this stand was maybe forty or fifty years old? He walked into the growth and looked around. While the trees seemed to have been planted haphazardly there was a small clear-ing, now overgrown with brush and smaller saplings. The clearing floor was scattered with brush, leaves, moss and twigs.

Patrick walked around the clearing in a spiral pat-tern, working slowly to the center, all the while using his metal-tipped walking stick to jab the ground; walking, jab-bing, searching, until the metal end of the walking stick finally resounded with a metallic clunk.

Down on his hands and knees, he cleared away the leaves. He eventually removed the surrounding forest debris to reveal a circle about one-meter in diameter. He used his walking stick to poke within the circle, every poke yielding the hollow, metallic clang. He'd discovered a metal man-hole, an access cover that had been permanently camouflaged.

He kicked the leaves back over the area to hide it. Perhaps he'd found the way Schleiman had accessed the bunker system. He needed to get back to the parking lot and meet Dieter. Tonight they would come back.

Thirty

Walther König sat with his associates in the restaurant and sullenly picked at his food. "Anything from the Stubers?"

Peter looked up and solemnly shook his head.

"Try again."

"Their phone is off, or the battery is dead, maybe it's lost, or…"

"TRY AGAIN," König growled.

Peter reached into his pocket, retrieved his cell phone and glumly called, "Nothing."

"Damn!" König slammed the table with his fist. He turned to Heinrich. "The Stubers, Kurt and Erich, is Deveraux killing them all? The woman in the alley, the one who killed Erich, did you see her?"

Heinrich Schiff set down his beer. "Not well, it happened too quickly, tall, blond, she moved fast and shot well, a professional."

König looked at the other two. "I'm almost certain that the man in the alley was Deveraux, but why the disguise, and was the woman *with* him, working for him?"

The other men answered him with silent, inquisitive looks.

Peter spoke. "Do you want me to go back up to Hamburg? Check on the Dominatrix friend of Deveraux, see if I can find out where the Stubers are?"

König thought for a moment. "No, let's stay together; see if we can retrace Schleiman's steps here in Berchtesgaden."

Heinrich finished his beer and signaled for another. "The authorities sealed off the tunnel where he died. We didn't find anything at his apartment. What can we expect to find here?"

König drummed his fingers on the table. "They went in and dug out Schleiman's body through the traditional bunker system entrance. What if Schleiman found another way in, maybe through an unknown or forgotten section?"

The other two looked doubtful. "We found no maps at Kessler's, he didn't give us any information we could use," Peter said.

König grudgingly nodded his agreement with that assessment. "Agreed, but for now we stay here, take a walk around the *Obersalzberg*, and keep our eyes open for Deveraux."

"And the woman from the alley," Heinrich added.

Thirty One

Dieter and Patrick sat in the corner booth of a *Gästehaus* on the outskirts of Berchtesgaden. While they waited for their meals Patrick showed Dieter where he found the tunnel entrance. "Right here, just a bit off the trail, in some trees," he pointed to a spot on the map, "exactly where Schleiman marked it."

Dieter studied the map and drank his beer.

Patrick continued, "I'd be willing to bet that it was some kind of emergency, or auxiliary entrance or exit, something that only a few knew about. They probably planted the trees around there when they put it in."

"Maybe Kessler knew about it, maybe one of the few who did," Dieter added.

"Yea, that's what I'm betting. When Schleiman got tipped off to the lost document, the important last mission for the *Führer,* and the lost tunnel he put it all together, and..." Patrick let it hang.

Dieter snorted, "Doubtful, that's a big stretch, Patrick."

"I don't disagree, but it's not about what *we* believe; it's about what *they* believe. And they believe that there is something there, or was something, and whatever it was, it was worth killing for."

"*Ja*," Dieter pulled out the photos provided by Angelika.

Patrick studied them closely. "This one's König all right, he was the one who contacted me at the *München Marienplatz*. This one," he pointed to Erich Güler, "was the one who met me in Rothenburg and who led me into the alley."

"The one Steffi killed," Dieter dryly added.

Patrick smiled, "Thankfully."

Dieter tapped a large index finger on the picture of Kurt Rothe. "This one breaks into Hannelore's house." He and Patrick exchanged a silent look; they hadn't asked many details about what had happened to the man, but each of them imagined the worst.

Patrick thought for a moment. "Hannelore said that there were four and König, for a total of five. We have seven pictures here, so either there are more men involved—"

"I think König and four," Dieter interjected. "Hannelore found out all the man knows."

"The Stubers? Maybe an afterthought? When the break-in at Hannelore's failed?"

Dieter nodded in the affirmative.

"OK," Patrick said, "I'm inclined to agree. So of these four remaining pictures, let's assume that two of them are out there somewhere, working with König. We need to memorize the rest of these faces. The first one to spot the enemy has a decided advantage."

Their meals came and they quietly put away the maps and pictures. Patrick slowly ate and took in the ambience of the charming *Gästehaus*. *Yes, a nice Bavarian dinner, and then a night-time hike.*

Thirty Two

Patrick and Dieter reached the small grove of trees shortly after midnight. It didn't take long for the two of them to pull up the metal access cover. They were greeted with the dank smell of the tunnel.

Now the dark opening lay before them. They waited quietly to see if anyone was nearby, or following them. As expected, the area was lonely and deserted at this early hour of the morning.

Dieter let his flashlight play on the dark hole beneath them. The shaft was thirty feet down, with metal hand holds embedded in the concrete. The handholds looked to be recently used, the covering of dirt and vegetation on them smudged. Dieter gestured with his light; and Patrick started down the shaft.

The hand holds seemed solid, if slick with moss, and Patrick proceeded cautiously, with Dieter using his flashlight to provide lighting. When Patrick reached the bottom they once more turned off the lights and remained silent for a few seconds. Again, they were alone.

With an 'all clear' from Patrick, Dieter descended.

As expected, they found the tunnel long, dark and dank smelling. It was surprisingly spacious, even Dieter could stand fully up-right. Their flashlights played along the sides and floor. The floor revealed that someone else had been here, and recently. The footprints and tracks left in patches of water, mud, and moss were recent.

Dieter shined his flashlight along the tracks, following them up the length of the tunnel until they disappeared from sight. He turned to Patrick, "Schleiman?"

"That'd be my guess. He probably thought he'd found some kind of lost cache of…something. It doesn't look like anyone had been here before him."

They studied their surroundings for a moment: a long straight concrete tunnel, with wires and pipes along the length, near the roof.

Dieter played his light over the wires and pipes, "Electric, lights, alarms, communications?"

"Probably, if it was me I'd sure have lights down here, and some kind of alarm to tell me when that hatch above was breached. Well, let's see where it goes."

They walked down the tunnel, their lights illuminating their way ahead, their footfalls echoing off the concrete walls. It was hard to tell an exact direction, but Patrick guessed they were proceeding north, in the direction of the *Platterhof* Hotel, and the major parts of the *Obersalzberg* Nazi bunker complex. The hiking trail had been approximately five hundred meters south of the *Platterhof*, but he didn't know how far they had come. They walked quietly, finally arriving at a heavy metal door. The door looked like it had been sealed for some time, decades, and only recently opened. There was evidence of chiseling and cutting with a metal torch. It hadn't been a clean job, but someone had managed to open what had probably once been a heavy, blast-type door.

Patrick and Dieter looked at the door, and then at each other.

Dieter scowled, "Amateur work, too fast, no skill."

"Yea, want to bet that the main bunker system is on the other side of this?"

Dieter shrugged and put his bulk to the door. The rusty hinges creaked, and the door opened.

They were in the main bunker complex, of that Patrick was sure, but exactly where, he had no idea. The faint footprints they had followed the entire course were visible in the main tunnel as well, veering off to the right. With a silent look to each other, Patrick and Dieter started down the tunnel, following the footprints.

As they walked, their flashlights beamed across the floors and walls. Decades of ground water leakage formed stalactites from the ceiling, turning their environment into a kind of modern-day, surrealistic, man-made cavern. Faded painted directions and signage in German could still be seen on the walls, relics from the days when this complex served as a refuge for the National Socialist Party elite: Hitler, Göring, and Bormann.

Dieter pointed his flashlight to the roof, the beam illuminating tree roots pushing their way through. Below them, on the floor, lay pieces of plaster and cement. He shook his head, "What the British Lancasters couldn't do with bombs, a few trees..."

It wasn't long before they came to a pile of rubble, the passage collapsed, and further progress blocked. They stepped forward and examined the wreckage. It was recent.

"Want to bet they recovered Schleiman's body from the other side?"

Dieter agreed, "No sign of anyone else on this side."

Patrick threw his hands up in disgust. He turned in a circle, examining the walls with his flashlight. "We got nothing."

"*Nichts*," Dieter agreed.

Patrick tried to think. "OK, Schleiman found an unused, or unknown entrance, got into the bunker system, *thought* he had found something, and got killed and buried trying to get at it."

"*Ja*, I agree."

"Think there's anything else to see here?"

Dieter gave a contemptuous laugh.

The two men stood silent for a moment, playing their lights over the various surfaces. Finally they turned, looked at each other and started back the way they came.

Thirty Three

König and his associates sat around the breakfast table. The dishes had been cleared away, and they finished their coffee. König looked at Karl Harth. "Any contact with the Stubers in Hamburg?"

Karl shook his head, "Nothing."

"Has anyone seen the woman from the alley in Rothenburg, or Deveraux?"

Karl and Heinrich looked at König and shook their heads.

König looked down at the table and sighed. "So we don't know where the Stubers are, who killed Erich, or where Deveraux is, right?" He was greeted with a murmured reply. He finished his coffee, "Let's drive up to the *Obersalzberg*, see if we can find anything."

Heinrich grimaced. "Again? Look for what? *What* are we looking for?"

"I don't know!" König spat, "Deveraux, the woman, a clue to where Schleiman was searching, something!"

He rose and stormed out of the restaurant.

The other two exchanged worried and confused looks, and followed him out.

*****

They'd arrived early at what they thought would be a good vantage point to watch people coming and going from the main tourist area on the *Obersalzberg*. Patrick remained in the car, as his was the face König and his men might recognize. Dieter was out and about in the tourist areas.

Luck was with them. They hadn't waited more than an hour when Patrick saw the car with König and his associates. He called Dieter, "They just drove by, König, Harth… The other one looks to be… Heinrich Schiff."

Dieter heard Patrick shuffling papers. "OK, I'll watch for them. If they split up do we take one?"

Patrick's reply was grim, "Yes, we're going to end this."

*****

König looked around while the other two awaited instructions. "The authorities said that Schleiman was seen hiking from here, and people in the shops said that they sold him water and snacks. He wasn't up here on holiday. Something in this area was the key." König pointed to two hiking trails. "Take a walk; see if you can see anything unusual. Watch for Deveraux and the woman."

Heinrich and Karl shook their heads and started for their respective paths.

*****

Dieter was on the phone to Patrick, "They split up."

"Yea, I see. Let's take Harth, the trail he's on looks like it has fewer people." Patrick saw Dieter turn, and follow in Karl Harth's direction. He got out of the car and followed at a distance.

With his long legs Dieter easily caught up with Harth, while Patrick held back, just out of sight.

Dieter fell in step beside his quarry, and beamed a smile, "*Gruß Gott*!"

Karl Harth replied with a nod of the head and his own, *"Gruß Gott.." Bavarians!*

Dieter smiled again, "You look for Herr Schleiman?"

Karl Harth was immediately on guard, his right hand reaching for his gun, but he wasn't fast enough. Dieter landed a heavy blow to Karl's midsection doubling him over. Dieter followed with a second body shot to the kidneys. Before Karl collapsed, Dieter held him up.

Patrick ran up, he and Dieter held Karl between them, walking him back to the parking lot. A family of English tourists stopped to ask if there was a problem. Patrick smiled, thanked them, and told them their friend had eaten some bad eggs that morning.

Dieter reached around and removed the gun from Karl. Patrick quickly patted him down, finding and removing a cell phone, spare ammunition clip, and a silencer for the gun. He pocketed the cell phone, giving the ammo clip and silencer to Dieter.

Patrick leaned in to whisper to the man. "We're

going somewhere to talk, don't make any trouble, and you might live through this."

Dieter ran ahead to see if the way to the car was clear. He didn't see König or Heinrich, and he signaled Patrick to bring Karl to the car. They got in, Dieter driving, and Patrick and Karl in the back. Karl was still clutching his side. Patrick almost winced from the look on the man's face, imagining Dieter's huge fist pummeling the body.

Patrick told Dieter, "Drive someplace quiet, private."

Although Dieter had no familiarity with the area, he eventually managed to navigate the rental car onto a little used road that led into a secluded backwoods.

*****

Walther König grabbed his cell phone and called Heinrich, "Anything?"

"*Nein.*"

"Keep looking. We'll stay here a while longer and then figure out what to do next." König ended the call and dialed Karl.

*****

Dieter backed the car into the small forest access road, ready to leave quickly, if needed.

Patrick turned to Karl, "What are you looking for?"

Karl still held his side, but grunted, "The Will, the fucking Will! You know that. You were paid to get it."

"Why does König want it, if it even exists?"

Karl realized his situation was precarious. Erich was dead, Kurt was dead, the Stubers most probably so. He didn't want to be next. "He wants to sell it, money, it's all for money."

"Sell it to who?"

"Arabs, I was with him when we met with one of them. They offered big money for König to get Hitler's real Last Will and Testament."

"Why, why would Arabs give a shit about a lost Nazi document?"

"Stir up a new Neo Nazi climate, more anti-Semitism; they can have another front for terrorism."

Patrick shook his head, it was all too bizarre. "What makes anyone think that there was ever a second Will and Testament?"

"Arab journalist, he interviewed Hanna Reitsch at a gliding school she ran in Ghana, after the war. She told him of seeing this Major in the bunker, that he had a special meeting with Hitler, then he was mysteriously sent on a personal mission for the *Führer*, south, some say to Bavaria, some say to the bunkers here, on the *Obersalzberg*."

Patrick looked at Dieter.

Dieter shrugged with a 'hell, I don't know, could be' gesture.

Patrick looked back at Karl. "Does König believe that there 'is' a Will?"

Karl laughed, and winced when he did, "König believes that the Arabs have two million to pay for it."

"Why did König kill Kessler, and send one of his men to Hamburg?"

"We thought that Kessler might know where

Schleiman was looking, or even if he'd found it. You? The thing in Hamburg, it was to keep you in our pocket. If you got the will for König, maybe he pays you, maybe he kills you. If we get the will, we save your cut."

"Money," Patrick said derisively.

Karl nodded, "Money."

Patrick was silent; he'd done jobs for money, dirty jobs, wet work, *All for money*.

"How did Schleiman figure in on this?"

"He was supposedly on a dig in Arabia, some old site, and happened to talk to the same Arab reporter who interviewed Reitsch. He got the same story, contacted his old friend Kessler who worked on the tunnels, tried to figure out if there was a last redoubt, a last Nazi refuge. Find the will, get the glory."

"What's König doing now?"

Karl looked at Patrick. "He looks for clues, for the Will—for you."

Patrick returned the look, "Get out of the car."

*****

König hit the SEND button to call Karl, and cursed when no one picked up the call. He called Heinrich, "Get back here, we have problems."

*****

Karl slowly exited the car.

Patrick looked at him from the open door. "Get lost, lose yourself, don't come back."

Dieter quickly turned from his position in the front

seat. "Patrick! Never leave an enemy in your rear!"

Patrick was quiet for a moment, then stepped out of the car and walked to Karl, looking him in the eyes. "Your friend, Kurt, in Hamburg, is dead. The man in Rothenburg—dead. The Stubers—dead. The next time I see you, it's the last day of your life."

Before Karl could reply or respond Patrick shot him in the leg, shattering his right knee cap.

"What is it with you Irish and kneecapping?" Dieter asked when Patrick returned to the car.

"*Irish* father, *French* mother," Patrick replied, "and next time, I'll hear him coming."

Thirty Four

Patrick and Dieter sat at an outside table at a local beer garden. Dieter took a long pull from a dark beer and smacked his lips. "I don't think you're getting 250,000 Euros from *Herr* König."

"You don't think so?" Patrick drank his own beer. He looked at the cell phone on the table, willing it to ring. It did, the display illuminated with 'König.' He flipped it open, put it to his ear, and heard the voice.

"Karl? Karl?"

Patrick spoke slowly and deliberately, "We need to meet," and was greeted with silence. He could imagine König grinding his teeth; he felt the malice from the other end of the phone. The voice that came back dripped with venom.

"Dev-er-aux. You have the document?"

Patrick chuckled, König didn't even ask about his man. The job, the payoff, that was all that mattered. Everything and everyone else was expendable. Patrick knew it all too well, that's why he'd left it behind, or so he'd thought. "A meeting—you—alone." Again, silence.

König cursed under his breath. Karl was now a casualty, obviously. *How much did Deveraux know; did he know about Heinrich? His intelligence was good. Is he working for someone?* "Do you have the document?"

Patrick paused, "*Herr* König, *why* did you send a man to Hamburg? Didn't trust me to hold up my end?"

"Insurance, at one time you may have done the same."

Patrick paused; König was right on that one, at one time he may have played it the same way, but taking women? That was never Patrick's style; even rogues had standards. He repeated his demand, "A meeting, just the two of us."

"You have the document?" König asked.

"You have the money?"

An uneasiness silence passed as each man realized that they could attend the meeting empty-handed, and leave the same way. Patrick broke the silence, "*Kehlsteinhaus*, this afternoon, be on the last group that comes up—come alone."

The line went dead.

"Doesn't give him, or us, much time," Dieter said.

"We don't need much time, and I don't want to give him any time to put someone in place. I'll meet with König, you watch for Heinrich."

"You don't think he comes alone?"

Patrick surveyed the street, scanning his environment. "No, I don't think he'll come alone, not his style. But he doesn't know exactly how much we know, whether or not we've made his men. That's our advantage."

Hitler's Will

Dieter dropped Euros on the table to pay for their beers. He pulled the picture of Heinrich from his pocket and looked at it again, showing it to Patrick. Both men burned the image into their mind.

"I'll take Karl's gun and silencer," Patrick said. "If I have to use them, I'll leave them at the scene; I don't know where they came from, but they can't trace them back to us. Watch my back."

Dieter gave Patrick the weapon, put the photograph in his pocket, and walked away.

The two men made their way separately back to the *Obersalzberg*, Dieter taking the car and Patrick going by bus.

At the *Obersalzberg-Hintereck* Patrick booked himself on one of the buses that would make the winding climb up the scenic *Kehlsteinstraße* to Hitler's Eagle's Nest. He watched as Dieter purchased another disposable camera, playing the picture-taking tourist in this idyllic Bavarian setting. He wondered if Dieter had any other ruse at his disposal, then again, the picture-taking tourist worked well in these locales. Patrick smiled, *Does he really get those pictures developed, does he have a photo album at home?* The bus came and Patrick was one of the last to board, scanning each passenger, looking for possible enemies.

Patrick was arriving early to scout out his egress route and find a good place to wait for König. On the way up the mountain he relaxed, listening to the multi-lingual story of the mountain road and the 'oohs and ahhs' of the camera-wielding tourists.

At the summit, Patrick took his time familiarizing

himself with the area and the location of the hiking trail he planned to take back down the mountain-alone. Satisfied with his reconnaissance he made his way down the tunnel to the elevator that would take him to *Kehlsteinhaus*, Hitler's Eagle's Nest.

He felt a chill when he stepped inside the elevator with its rich brass appointments. *The same elevator used by Hitler, Bormann and the rest; the very architects of this bloody endeavor that's consumed me.* A line from Shakespeare popped into his head, 'The evil that men do lives after them'. Patrick shook off the morbid thoughts and focused on the task at hand; he found a table in the restaurant, one that gave him a good view of the room, and waited for his adversary.

König entered, scanned the room, and found Patrick. He pulled out a chair, "Eva Braun's former tea room, a bit ironic, considering our quest." König waited for his coffee to come, adding sugar and cream before he spoke again. "You have the document?"

Patrick was direct, "No. I don't believe the document ever existed. I'm still not certain why you hired me."

König slowly stirred his coffee. "*You* were the one the client wanted." He shrugged, "To me, you were a backup, a secondary measure. You've undertaken sensitive jobs in the past. Perhaps if there was a document you would recover it."

"And Kessler?"

"Ah… That was unfortunate; we hoped to learn something. Apparently he didn't know exactly what Schleiman was after, or exactly where he was looking. He was an old man, in the wrong place at the wrong time."

"Moving on the house in Hamburg, that was un-wise."

König forced a regrettable smile, "It appears so. We seem to have underestimated your colleagues. Who was the woman, in Rothenburg?" König nervously glanced around the room, fearing the deadly female may return.

Patrick didn't answer the question about Steffi. "Back to business, there's no lost Will, no such document."

Anger and denial flashed in König's eyes. "You are certain?"

"Yea, pretty sure about that, no document, never was."

*****

Dieter watched Heinrich drive by in the Mercedes and park. He continued to watch as Heinrich remained in the car. Dieter ambled in the car's direction, still playing the tourist. As he neared the car he saw Heinrich holding his hand to his ear, as if trying to hold in an ear piece. *Just like Rothenburg, König is probably wired, and Heinrich is listening to his conversation with Patrick.*

He took out his camera and walked forward, an-other casual, sightseeing tourist. He walked by the Mer-cedes, turning to take a picture of the mountains behind the car. After taking the picture he waved at Heinrich and smiled. Dieter held up his camera, gesturing and smiling, at the scene behind the car.

Heinrich turned to look at what the big man was waving and smiling about, but saw only the Alps against the blue sky. They were certainly scenic, but not particularly significant enough to get the large, blond man excited.

When Heinrich turned back, the man was directly beside the driver's-side window, and Heinrich found himself staring directly into the barrel of Dieter's Glock.

Dieter tapped on the glass, with his free hand, keeping the gun leveled. Heinrich flipped the switch to lower the window, and before the window was completely down Dieter shoved his huge fist through the opening, the single blow against Heinrich's face rendering him unconscious.

Dieter opened the door, pushing Heinrich to the side. With plastic tie-wraps from his pocket he quickly bound Heinrich's hands. He grabbed the earpiece, stuck it is his ear, put the car in gear and drove off. Through the metallic-sounding electronics he heard Patrick, "Yea, pretty sure about that, no document, never was."

Dieter pulled out his cell phone and called Patrick. The call was short, Dieter said, "I have him," and hung up.

*****

König watched Deveraux end the short call and put the phone away. He couldn't help but notice the smile that played across Deveraux's lips. "Something amuses you?"

"In a tragic-comic way, yes, I suppose so. We have Heinrich. I think it's time that we ended our business association; I'm going to need your Arab contacts."

"So you can sell the Will yourself?" König sneered.

Patrick leaned in, face to face with his adversary. "*Herr* König, there *is* no fucking Will." He rose, "Let's take a walk, discuss how we will end this."

They made their way silently to the elevator and then out the long tunnel onto the bus lot.

Hitler's Will

"Walk ahead of me," Patrick pointed, "over there, the hiking trail."

The two men quickly disappeared from the view of the throngs of tourists milling about and boarding buses.

"I didn't bring my hiking shoes," König said.

"That's the last thing you need to be concerned about. It's late in the day, and a long hike up this trail, I doubt we'll meet anyone coming up; keep walking." Patrick now had Karl's gun in his hand, "I'm going to need those names, your contacts."

"What do you intend to sell them? If there's no Will..."

"Simply tying up loose ends."

König stopped and spun around, "You don't know who you're dealing with, Deveraux." He saw the gun in Patrick's hand.

"Obviously *you* didn't, you got in over your head," Patrick said, "with both me *and* your employers." Patrick quickly looked around to insure they were alone. "We're not going to have a lengthy negotiation; I want the names, contacts. Give me what I want, and you may get off this mountain alive."

"This isn't over between us," König handed Patrick his cell phone, "it's under Will, call that number." König's eyes burned with hate, "It's not over."

Patrick lifted the gun and pulled the trigger as König's forehead erupted in an explosion of blood and bone. "Yes, with us, it *is* over."

Thirty Five

"Have a nice walk?" Dieter handed Patrick a bottle of water.

"It was all downhill," Patrick took a drink, "I'm thankful for that."

Dieter peered down the trail, "You come alone?"

"König's still up there, he won't be coming down, left him in a ditch, covered with some brush. Some hikers will undoubtedly find him, but we'll be halfway to Hamburg by then."

The men settled into Dieter's car. "So, it's over? Or is there more?"

Patrick held König's cell phone, "I'm about to find out." He brought up the phone's menu and punched the number under 'Will'.

The number rang several times before it was answered by a heavily accented voice, "König?"

Patrick's Irish eyes twinkled as he looked at Dieter and answered, "König is dead, his associates are dead.

This is Deveraux. You want the Will, you deal with me."

Moments of silence passed before a new voice came on the line. This voice had the same Middle-Eastern accent, but was more refined and cultured. "Deveraux, I am not surprised at this turn of events. You have the Will?"

"I do, but my fee has gone up. I want the two million you promised König—and a million more."

Engaging laughter greeted Patrick's response. "Deveraux! An assassin *and* a capitalist!"

"The money," Patrick repeated "and *you* at the exchange."

Again, Patrick was greeted with silence.

"One week from today," the voice said.

Patrick listened as detailed information on the meet was relayed. He closed the phone.

"Well," Dieter asked, "where to next?"

"Can you and Steffi make a trip with me?"

"To?"

"Marseille."

Thirty Six

Dieter pulled the car onto yet another small side street and parked. A recent rain shower left everything wet. Against the black and cloudy night the streetlamps cast rays of glistening light from pools of water. "We'll walk from here; the docks begin a block south."

Patrick and Steffi got out of the car and met Dieter at the trunk. While Dieter and Patrick filled their pockets with the items they would need, they watched as Steffi opened the case containing the DSR 1 sniper rifle. She expertly checked each piece and slipped it into specially made pockets of her khaki swing coat.

Patrick nodded his approval; with her tall frame and Nordic good looks, a casual onlooker would not notice the coat didn't fit perfectly. "You've done this before?"

She smiled her reply and brushed back her hair.

"I was here this afternoon, mingling with the crew of a freighter," Dieter began his reconnaissance report as the group walked up the deserted street. "The meeting place is by one of the piers. I'm betting they're coming in by boat; from someplace out in the Mediterranean. There's a crane a hundred meters down the dock. From there Steffi will have a clear field of fire for the meet." Dieter suddenly halted, holding up his hands to stop those behind him. "There's someone up there."

Patrick moved by Dieter to peer around the corner. Blocking their path was a solitary figure. Even from a distance Patrick could tell that beneath his jacket the lone guard was carrying some kid of weapon. Patrick looked up and down the street, "What about going around, approaching from a different way?"

"Maybe," Dieter replied, "but that still leaves him in our rear."

"There's no cover to approach him from here, he'd spot us before we could take him out without a disturbance or him sounding an alarm."

"If we circled around the block, and came—"

"*Scheisse!* Men and their plans."

Patrick and Dieter turned to see the cursing Steffi thrust her coat into Patrick's hands. Reaching back she tugged at the clip holding up her hair, the golden mane falling to her shoulders. She reached up and unbuttoned the three top buttons on her blouse. A surprised Patrick and Dieter watched as she reached into her blouse to pull her breasts up and outwards, the lace of her bra now easily revealed in the cleavage of her half undone blouse. Her last act was to drop her head forward and back up, making her hair full and wild looking. She reached into Dieter's jacket, removing the Sykes-Fairbairn knife and holding it out to him. "I'll turn him around, do it when he has his back to you." She ran her tongue over her lips and pinched her cheeks. With a final shake of her hair Steffi confidently and seductively walked into the narrow street.

The guard immediately turned to see the figure coming into the light. He reached inside his coat for his weapon, but relaxed as the tall and beautiful woman approached him.

"Marseille, these fucking docks! My boyfriend says he will take me to France and we end up here." Steffi walked past the guard, his eyes and body following her, as she'd planned. She turned to the direction she'd come, facing towards Dieter and Patrick, and the guard moved with her, his back now exposed. She moved close and leaned forward, exposing her ample cleavage, "Have a cigarette?"

Her quarry fumbled in his pockets for a cigarette and lighter. When he struck the flame she gently wrapped her hand around his, pulling him closer to her.

Dieter's long legs quickly closed the gap enough to insure an accurate strike and the Sykes commando knife flew from his hand. As Steffi pulled the lighter and hand closer to her face she saw the man's eyes grow wide when the knife plunged into his back. Her free hand went to the man's mouth, muffling any cry as she moved close to hold up his body. Dieter came forward and helped her place the body in a nearby doorway.

Dieter slid the knife back in its sheath and took a radio from the dead body. "He was obviously in contact with someone. We can listen, but it may not do much good if they're speaking in Arabic."

"Yea," Patrick agreed, "I only know a few phrases, but we'll monitor it anyway."

Steffi pointed up the street, "Wait here, I'll go and see if there is anyone else."

When Steffi came back she had her hair back up and was buttoning her blouse. She took her coat from Patrick. "There's no one around, he was probably the only one, someone here early to secure the meeting place. I saw the crane, it looks like a good position."

"OK," Patrick said, "get in position. From there you should be able to see them, or their advance party come in. Dieter and I will wait back at the corner and approach just prior to the meeting time. Let's make a final comm check."

All three checked their earpieces and did a quick check of their individual radio communications. Affirmative nods all around indicated that everything was good.

Patrick looked at the others. "OK, let's get in position and get this over with." Without another word Steffi gave each of them a quick kiss and set off down the street. Patrick and Dieter watched her walk out of sight.

Steffi quickly climbed the crane and used a pry bar to open the door to the operator's cab. There wasn't much room, but she quickly assembled the sniper rifle and readied her position.

Finally their earpieces crackled with static and Steffi's voice, "I'm in place. I'm using the night vision, but don't see anything. Will let you know when someone approaches."

Dieter acknowledged her communication as he and Patrick took their positions in an alley. Patrick looked at his watch; this was the hard part, the laying in wait, but it gave them the advantage.

Their radios crackled with Steffi's voice. "There's

a boat that's come in to view several hundred yards off shore. It's big, a yacht, just lying there, minimal running lights."

"Acknowledged," whispered Dieter.

Suddenly the other earpiece was flooded with a stream of Arabic. Dieter handed it to Patrick who listened intently but shook his head. "I've no idea what they are saying, but it sounds excited."

They heard Steffi's voice in their ears, "The yacht launched a helicopter, it's coming this way." Steffi grabbed a tarp from the floor and pulled it over her, huddling as much as she could on the floor, out of site. Suddenly the crane cab was filled with light and dust as the helicopter hovered nearby, sweeping the area with a searchlight, it's blades churning up dust and making the crane sway. Just as quickly the helicopter pulled away, moving to survey the dock meeting area.

Steffi peeked out from the tarp and watched the helicopter flying back to the yacht. She adjusted her night-vision goggles, "Small craft launched from the yacht, inbound to our location, looks like the copter was to inspect the meet area."

For the last time Patrick looked at his watch, "OK, let's go." He and Dieter left the alley, walked down the street and out onto the docks.

Steffi's voice was reassuring. "I have you in sight, no one else on the docks, looks like everyone is coming in from the boat. I have five targets on the boat."

Dieter responded, "Patrick and I will deal with the ones at the meet. You'll have to take anyone who stays with the boat or shows up from somewhere else." He took a deep breath of the sea air as they emerged onto the barren dock. For Dieter this was as good a place as any for the final confrontation. He now heard the incoming boat and within moments it was visible. He and Patrick moved apart as they watched the boat tie up and three people climb up the ladder and onto the dock.

Steffi, with the benefit of a night vision telescopic sight was their eye in the sky. "Two left in the boat, looks like handguns and maybe an MP5 and HK. The three on the dock… I don't see anything large on them."

Patrick gave a slight nod of the head to acknowledge her transmission.

The three men stood silently for a moment opposite Dieter and Patrick before the one in the middle, in the expensive suit, spoke. "Do you know who I am?"

Patrick nodded, "Ja'bar al-Zubair, international financier of terrorists."

Zubair laughed, "And are you yourself not a terrorist Mr. Deveraux? An ex-IRA assassin?"

"We fight for different things, at different times."

Zubair seemed to consider this; the men on each side of him staring at Patrick and Dieter. "*Herr* König was greedy. He underestimated you. I never did, it was always my plan that you would bring the document to me, that *I* would stand before the infamous Patrick Deveraux."

"Sorry to disappoint you, but there is no document, never was. It's myth, legend."

"A pity, I don't have the Will, and you don't get your Euros. It seems we have both lost."

"It seems so," Patrick waited, he sensed there was more.

"The Will was only half my prize. If I've lost that, I will still have my revenge for my nephew."

Patrick shifted his weight as he heard Steffi, "One out of the boat, in the water, moving to your right."

Dieter heard the warning as well, marking as his targets the two men on either side of al-Zubair. His earpiece sounded with Steffi's voice, "Target climbing up the dock, fifty meters to your right, has an AK. It's a set-up. When I have a clear shot I'm taking it, first him, then the one in the boat."

"Your nephew double-crossed us, stole from us. It was a legitimate sanction," Patrick said. "He paid the price for his treachery."

Al-Zubair's face grew livid. "*You* speak of treachery…"

A shot rang out and a man screamed. As quickly another shot split the night air. The two men with al-Zubair looked to their left and back to the boat, where the shots and screams originated. That split second distraction cost them their lives. Dieter pulled his Glock and killed the first man as he was reaching for his gun. The second man was able to draw his weapon when Dieter's second shot dropped him on the spot.

Patrick had his Glock out as well, pointed at al-Zubair, who stood defiantly and motionless before him.

Steffi's voice came over their earpieces, "All clear, no one else in sight."

Dieter did a three-sixty, his weapon outstretched, surveying the docks. "Clear."

"It seems that perhaps I, also underestimated you," al-Zubair spat. "You've caused me much trouble Deveraux. I wish *you'd* been in the car when my men ran it off the road."

Patrick felt a flush of pain, sadness and anger well

up within him. *Heike, my beloved Heike, was murdered in an attempt at revenge? She died because of an act committed by me?*

Al-Zubair smiled, "You didn't know?"

"I do now." Patrick raised the Glock. "Yes, this is about vengeance." He pulled the trigger, not seeing the shattered face of al-Zubair. He saw his beloved Heike, blowing him a kiss as she drove off for the last time. Patrick heard her say, *Live my love, it's time to move on.*

He felt Dieter's hand on his shoulder, heard his voice, "Patrick, we must go."

Both men holstered their weapons and walked away from the docks, toward Steffi who waited at the alley.

"It is over, now?" Dieter asked.

"Yes," Patrick said.

"Good, I go back to the boat, to Mathias, to the sea, and you?"

"I'm taking a lady shopping for a coat."

Epilogue

27 May, 1945
Near Leonding, Austria

 Major Jürgen Strasser stirred, waking from a fitful sleep. He'd spent the night in a ditch on the outskirts of town, and his body was stiff from the cold, hard ground. He rummaged through his pockets, hoping to find something to eat, perhaps a piece of bread or sausage. Glumly he realized the futility of his search. He was tired and hungry; the last four weeks had taken everything he had.

Yes, they'd sent him on this 'fool's errand.' But he was a soldier, and given an order he would carry it out, or die in the attempt. He stood and stretched. The early morning sun was burning the haze from the fields. *Maybe someone will be planting here next year, when it's all over.*

He warily circled the outskirts of town, using the fields and forests as cover. For weeks he'd been on the move, and he no longer had any idea what cities or villages were controlled by the Allies, especially the hated Russians. Today Leonding seemed quiet.

He found a place where he could observe the small cemetery and he settled down to wait for dusk. His stomach growled, but his soldier's will and discipline kept him in place. *Finish this one last mission, find some food, and then disappear, walk away.*

That was his plan. For him it would be over. In his travels from Berlin he'd heard rumors that the surrender documents were already signed, the *Führer* was dead. It was hard to know the truth.

As the sun set he crept from his hiding place, and walked into the cemetery, trying to appear as another of the many mourners of the war dead. *I am, I've lost many comrades in years of hard and bitter fighting.*

He walked among the markers, searching in the fading light for the name that would finish his quest. Finally he saw it: Klara Hitler.

He knelt beside the modest grave and reached in his pocket for the envelope so carefully guarded on his long trek from Berlin. From the envelope he removed the simple soldier's Iron Cross 1st Class. He'd been told that it was awarded for 'personal bravery and general merit' in World War One. *World War One, now we number our wars!*

From his battle tunic he pulled out his *SS* dagger and dug in the earth near the headstone, making a small hole in the damp soil. He reverently placed the Iron Cross in the hole, pulled the dirt back on top, and packed it down.

For a few moments he knelt before the marker, his eyes closed, his breathing slowed. He picked up a handful of earth and squeezed it in his fist. *How many of my comrades have died, their last thoughts of home and family? This is my last mission. For me the war is over, this soldier's life is over, my duty is finished.*

He rose to his feet and looked around; the cemetery was deserted, he was alone. He dusted off his shabby uniform, walked out, and stood at the entrance. The dagger in his hand felt heavy. He sighed, dropped the dagger to the ground, and stepped into the night.

About the Author

Greg Causey is an author and musician. He lived in Europe and visited many of the places in Hitler's Will. His other books include *Dancing With Natasha* and *Denizens of the Desert*.

The author can be reached at his web site:

www.gregcausey.com

Other Books
by
Gregory 'Greg' Causey

Dancing With Natasha

Dancing With Natasha takes the reader from "I Can't Dance," to "I'm A Dancing Machine." Greg and co-author Natasha detail the often agonizing, but always rewarding endeavor of learning Ballroom Dance. In this engaging, witty and poignant memoir, Greg and his wife, Joan make the trek to the Arthur Murray Dance Studio in Dayton, Ohio, for a few lessons to better enjoy the professional formal functions they attend. What they find is nothing short of miraculous.

In her own exuberant style, Natasha, their Russian instructress, explains how she moves beginners who consider the 'obligatory grope' on the floor to be dancing, to graceful self-expression. With the foreword written by Barbara Haller, Four-time United States Professional Theatrical Arts champion, and details from other students, instructors, and dance pros, *Dancing With Natasha* gives the reader an uncommon peek into this incredibly popular and exciting endeavor.

Print: 978-1-934446-00-3
E-Book: 978-1-934446-14-0

Denizens of the Desert: AMARC Photographs By Danny Causey

(Edited by Greg Causey)

Danny Causey parked his vehicle at the end of a row of B-52s, put on his sunglasses and pulled on his cap to shield his eyes from the relentless Arizona sun. He walked down endless rows of aircraft, the only sounds the gravel and scrub crunching under his work boots, maybe the scurry of a rabbit, the creaking of massive elevators and rudders in the hot desert wind and the occasional roar of a jet from nearby Davis Monthan Air Force Base.

For most of the aircraft, this was their last landing, the last stop in storied histories. They would be cannibalized for spare parts, or cut up and reclaimed for their metals. A special few might find refuge in museums or displays. One lone man would walk their ranks, photograph them and bid them a last goodbye. That's how this book came to be, these are the AMARC photographs of Danny Causey.

Denizens of the Desert contains photographs from the collection of former Aerospace Maintenance And Regeneration Center (AMARC) employee Danny Causey. Chapters are devoted to aircraft nose art found on B-52, KC-135, A-10 and F-111 aircraft. Additional chapters include photographs of other AMARC aircraft and a chapter on U.S. Navy aircraft at AMARC. Danny Causey was a USS Midway veteran.

ISBN: 978-193-4446-15-7